The Road Beast's Saga

Hippo

Kimberly Smith

Edited by Aria J.

This is a work of fiction. Names, characters, businesses, places, events, and incidents are either the products of the author's imagination or used in a fictitious manner. Any resemblance to actual persons, living or dead, or actual persons living or dead, or actual events is purely coincidental.

This adult contemporary romance is recommended for readers 18+ due to mature content.

February 2023 Edition

Chapter One

~Hippo~

It had been a week since Sameera broke into Bunker's office, and he hadn't seen her much. She spent most of her days training with Warthog and Mike, training. When she came home, they spent half an hour together having dinner. It would have been a great time to talk, except Hippo could see how tired she was, so he refrained from asking too many questions about her life before meeting him. After dinner, Sameera would go to her room to rest, after dinner, and Hippo wouldn't see her again until the next evening. Before leaving the following morning, she ensured he had something to eat that didn't require cooking.

He was thrilled when he woke up to delicious smells from the kitchen on Saturday. It was nearly noon, but the smells he inhaled were breakfast foods. He cleaned himself up, and made sure that his beard was trimmed. He needed a haircut, but that would have to wait until he could arrange for his barber to come by the house. He splashed a bit of cologne on before returning to the bedroom. It took him a little time to put on a pair of sweatpants Sameera had cut the left leg off of for him.

Hippo rested for a few minutes before searching for the food that made his mouth water. Stopping in the doorway to the kitchen, he watched Sameera for a few minutes. He felt like a pervert staring at her smooth caramel legs and thighs. His eyes rose, taking in the soft curve of her buttocks. She wore a pair of shorts with a matching short-sleeved hoodie in a coral color that looked great with her skin and dark hair up in a messy bun.

He hadn't tried to kiss her again. He wanted to kiss her, but it seemed she hadn't been ready for that since she pulled away from him that night. Now he felt like a boy with his first crush, unsure what to do to let her know he was into her. Hippo's instinct told him to be patient. Sameera liked him. He was sure of that, but something was holding her back from committing to exploring their attraction to each other. *Maybe she just thinks of me as a handsome friend.* "Morning," he said, moving into the kitchen.

She turned away from the stove, smiling brightly. "Hey. The food is almost ready. How are you feeling today?"

"Good. I'm not in nearly as much pain, so I'm not taking my pain pills as frequently and not napping as much. Do you have training today?" He moved around the counter, trying to find a spot where he could see her face.

"No, Mike and Warthog are giving me a few days to recuperate. I don't have to go back until Monday." She moved from the stove to the counter with the pan in her hands. "After breakfast, I thought we might get some fresh air. We could take a walk. You've been stuck in the house since coming home from the hospital. Is there somewhere you'd like to go?"

Hippo rubbed his hand over his hair. "I could use a haircut, but I'd need to call my barber and see if he can fit me in."

"Okay."

"I'll shoot him a text after we eat," he said, licking his lips as she put the bacon on their plates.

When she finished, Sameera picked up both plates and moved to the dining room. Hippo followed her, taking his usual spot at the head of the table. "What do you want to drink?"

Looking at the pancakes, he answered. "Milk."

Alright, I'll be back with that and the syrup in a minute."

Chapter Two

~Sameera~

She woke up happy to have some time off from training. Mike was wearing her out, but it was worth it. Yesterday during their session, she got the upper hand and flipped him onto his back. She spent the rest of her session with him grinning like a fool. Her gun training was going well too. Warthog had started her off cleaning the guns he supplied for general practice and shooting at his range. He had stressed the importance of knowing how to take apart, clean, and rebuild weapons to ensure they were in good working order. Next week she would actually start shooting. Warthog said he would let her try several until she found the one she was most comfortable with. Then she would work with that one most of the time, but he intended for her to train with several weapons. ***I'm starting to feel like a badass.***

She returned to the dining table with their drinks and the syrup. She grinned at Hippo as she entered.

He thought she hadn't heard him as he rolled into the kitchen, but she could always tell when he was near. It was like her body came to life around him. Since they almost kissed, her hormones were on overload. Sameera got a pulsating feeling in her body around him.

It was hard sitting with him every evening at dinner. She wanted him to attempt to kiss her again. She knew that she could initiate a kiss between them, but she felt too shy to do that. *I've screwed everything up, and I don't know how to get back to where we were.*

She had dressed in shorts to see if he would look at her with longing. Though her back had been to him, she felt warm and tingly everywhere his eyes touched. There was definitely a connection with him unlike anything she had ever experienced.

They didn't talk much while eating. Hippo moaned and made noises while he ate. To Sameera he sounded like he hadn't eaten in ages. "I take it that the food is good."

"Yes," he said, nodding his head. "I love pancakes and bacon."

"That's good to know," Sameera replied, smiling at him.

"I thought you didn't like having breakfast," Hippo said when he swallowed his food.

"I don't, but I like you, and you like breakfast," she said, picking up her milk. She watched the expression on his face go from a happy smile to something sultrier. *I wish I knew what you are thinking?*

The moment they were sharing was broken by the ringing of her phone. "Be right back." Sameera put her glass down and left the room. She had left a message for Eden when she woke up. Sameera hoped that's who was calling.

She grabbed the phone and swiped the green button without looking at the caller's information. "Hello?"

"Sameera, it's Eden."

"You got my message," she said excitedly.

"Yes. I was so glad to hear that you decided to make Dallas your home and that you were joining The Beasts. I called to invite you to a lady's lunch I'm having at my home tomorrow. It's last minute, but I want you to be here."

"I'd love to come. What time?"

"Noon. I've invited the girls from the club, my cousin, Tanya, and my sister Carla."

"Should I bring anything?"

"No. I've got everything covered, and we'll have a great time. It's casual dress, so wear whatever you're comfortable in. I'll see you tomorrow."

"I can't wait. Bye, Eden." She ended the call and returned to the dining room. She stopped inside the door, watching Hippo grab a slice of her bacon and shove it in his mouth.

"Sorry, but it was calling my name," he said, talking as he chewed.

Sameera sighed and shook her head. "Well, next time I'll take my plate with me." She snickered as she sat down.

"I'll make it up to you somehow," Hippo said, licking his lips.

Sameera tried not to stare, but it was hard not to. His lips were full and looked soft. *If you had let him kiss you, you'd know how they felt and tasted.* She wanted to tell her brain to shut up, but it was right.

"That was Eden. She invited me to have lunch at her house tomorrow."

Hippo stuck his bottom lip out, sulking. "So I have to have lunch alone tomorrow?"

"Isn't tomorrow the Super Bowl game?" Hippo nodded. "Why don't you have some of the Beasts over?"

Hippo smiled. "That's not a bad idea, but I bet most of them already have plans."

"Check with them. I can drop you off and pick you up after."

"Since I can't hang out with you, I will."

When they finished breakfast, Sameera took the dishes into the kitchen and rinsed them, putting them in the dishwasher. Hippo followed her. "When you're done, can you help me put on a shirt? I can't go out bare-chested."

"I'll be there in a minute," she told him as he left the room.

By the time Sameera entered Hippo's room, he was sitting near the closet with a button-up and a tee shirt on his lap. "My barber says he can fit me in if we get over there right now, but I can't decide which shirt will be easier to get on."

Sameera stood for a few seconds, thinking about the dynamics of putting each shirt on. "The button-down would be easier, I think. Let's get the sling off, but you have to hold your arm still while I put the shirt on you. Then we'll put the sling back in place."

"Okay."

Sameera unhooked the strap from him and slid the sling off. Then she carefully slid his shirt over his bad arm, making sure not to lift it. Within a few minutes, she was putting the sling back in place. "There, that wasn't so bad."

"Yeah, but now I look crazy," Hippo said, looking at his sweatpants.

"What about the shorts that I brought down? I think they will fit over your cast." Hippo moved the chair and pulled the shorts out of one of the drawers. "Do you need my help with those?"

Hippo raised his eyes to hers. "I think I can do it alone," his cheeks were filled with color.

Sameera couldn't keep the smile off her face. "Okay, I'll get my purse and move the car out of the garage. Meet me outside when you're ready."

Chapter Three

~Hippo~

Thinking of Sameera helping him change from his sweats to the shorts in his hand made the blood rush to his nether regions. He had told her that he slept naked, but he didn't tell her that since his accident, he hardly wore anything when he was alone. *I don't need to put them on to sit around the house.* She would have gotten a big surprise if she had stuck around to help him.

Hippo had never had trouble controlling his libido, but being around Sameera did something to him. He woke with a rock-hard dick, leaking fluid because she taunted him in his dreams. It started a few days after she moved in and was getting worse. Now, just being in the same room with her had him semi-hard. *I have to get my shit under control.*

Before changing his pants, Hippo found a pair of boxer briefs to put on first. The confinement should help him keep some control over his desires for Sameera. *It will only work if I stop looking at her. That's not going to happen. I can't keep my eyes off her. She's beautiful and not just physically.*

Sameera had a beautiful spirit. She was kind with a giving nature. She offered to help his mother with a church event to collect clothes, shoes, and blankets for the poor and homeless. It wasn't just her kindness. Sameera portrayed confidence and was understanding. She seemed at peace most of the time.

The only time he ever felt a hint of something else was when she got quiet. During those times, she seemed to be far away. When Hippo asked what she was thinking, she would smile and say she was thinking of her family. He asked about them, and it seemed to him that she had changed the subject each time. Because he respected her privacy, he didn't push, but it made him curious. Why wouldn't she talk about them?

Once he looked decent, Hippo gathered his wallet and phone and rolled through the house to meet Sameera in the driveway. He used the app on his phone to lock the door and set the alarm.

"Ready?" Sameera asked as she moved around the car to open the door for him.

"I am," he replied as he got into a position to move from the chair to the passenger seat. She thoughtfully moved the seat back to make room for his cast. Once settled in the seat, Sameera moved the wheelchair out of the way, leaning inside the car.

She grabbed the seatbelt, strapping him in. She smelled good. He caught a whiff of coconut and something else.

"How is that? Maybe you should ride in the back. That way, you won't have to wear a seatbelt."

When she turned her head to look at him, they were just inches apart. "God, you're beautiful," he said softly. She smiled and sent blood rushing from his brain to other parts of his anatomy. "I want to sit close to you. Just put the strap behind me." She did as Hippo asked, careful not to move his right shoulder or arm. She was so close that he felt the heat from her body. He turned his head towards her, kissing her cheek. "Thank you."

"For what?"

"Being you," Hippo said as she stood up.

She stepped out of the doorway. "Watch your arm."

She closed the door, moved the wheelchair around to the back of the vehicle, and lifted the lid of the trunk. She got the chair in, closed the trunk lid, and joined him in the car.

"I should have asked one of the guys to take me to the barber. I wasn't thinking about you lifting the chair in and out of the car."

Sameera started the engine and put her seatbelt on. She giggled. "I'm not a weakling. Yes, the chair is heavy, but I can handle it. Alright. Which way am I going?"

Hippo gave her instructions as she backed out of the driveway. There was no need for them to get on a highway. He directed her to take the surface streets into South Dallas. "I grew up near the barbershop. I've been getting my hair cut there since I was about ten."

"By the same guy?"

"Mr. Moon is in his eighties and has owned the shop since he opened it in the sixties. He still cuts hair, but his son, Malcolm, cuts my hair now that he is semi-retired. Malcom has his own shop in North Dallas, but one day a week, he comes to his father's shop to cut hair. Normally, I go to his shop off Northwest Highway."

As they turned onto the street where the shop was, Sameera smiled. "This isn't that far from Cougar's place."

"My mother's house isn't far from here either."

"Maybe we could go see her when we're done."

"I doubt she's at home, but I would like to drive by there afterward."

Chapter Four

~Sameera~

The space was much smaller than she expected. There was a small sitting area with a few worn old chairs, and a small flat-screen monitor was set to a sports station. They were greeted as soon as they crossed the threshold.

"Well, look-a-here," the man standing over his client said.

An older gentleman, whom Sameera guessed was Mr. Moon smiled and got up from one of the waiting area chairs. "Kenny, it's good to see you. I heard about what you and your club did rescuing those girls." He came closer and shook Hippo's hand. Then he raised his eyes to Sameera. "Who is this lovely lady? Is she your girlfriend?"

She couldn't see his face, but she believed Hippo was smiling. "I'm working on it."

"Hi, darling. I'm Morgan Moon."

Sameera took his hand, shaking it. "I'm Sameera."

"You can sit next to me," Mr. Moon said, smiling.

Hippo moved his chair. "You have to watch out for him. He's a ladies' man," Hippo said before turning his attention to Mr. Moon. "Don't be trying to steal my girl, old man."

Mr. Moon chuckled, "If I can take her from you, she was never yours, to begin with."

Sameera was tickled by his response and laughed with the other men in the shop. It was all good fun. Hippo smiled and nodded his head.

"Sameera, that's my son Malcolm and a longtime customer, Tony," Mr. Moon told her as they settled down side by side.

"Nice to meet you both," she said with a wave.

The next few minutes were interesting for her. Mr. Moon told her about the first time his father brought Hippo in for a haircut. "He must have been about three years old. Darren came in with his chest all puffed up. Kenny held onto his hand like D. would disappear if he let go." Sameera glanced at Hippo, whose chin rested against his chest as he shook his head. "When it was his turn to sit in the chair, he climbed on top of the phone books I had to use to raise him up and sat down like a G. He had a huge afro," Mr. Moon said, using his hands to show Sameera what he meant. "His hair probably added an extra pound or two to his weight. He looked so brave," he said, grinning at Hippo. "Until I turned on the clippers. He jumped out of that chair and started chanting, 'No. Don't like it, don't want it.' over and over again. In my whole life, I ain't never seen anyone move so fast. Before I could understand what was happening, he had climbed up on his father's lap and practically strangled him out of fear."

Sameera pressed her lips together, trying not to laugh as she stole a look at Hippo. It was the cutest story she had ever heard. Mr. Moon stood up. "Come with me, darling. I've got more pictures I can show you."

"Really, Mr. Moon?" Hippo said as the old man took Sameera by the hand and led her into the office at the back of the shop. She grinned at him as they moved away.

Mr. Moon pulled out a photo album and began flipping through it. "This may seem weird, but I have pictures of every child that had their first cut in this shop. Most of them still come here. Here is Kenny and his father."

Sameera looked at the photo. Hippo looked a lot like his father. He was smiling and happy as he stood in front of his dad with his freshly cut hair. "Adorable. He does look like him."

"Well, they say if you feed them long enough, they will start to look like you." Sameera wasn't sure what he meant by that, but he continued. "I knew his mother before she got out of the life and started going to church. She turned her entire life around when she got pregnant with Kenny's sister. She left their daddy and met D. They were happy for a long time, but it all changed after he got killed. Dottie didn't know what to do. Everyone respected D. for raising those kids like they were his own. When D. died, Kenny took it really hard. Then his sister was snatched off the street on her way home from school, and Kenny seemed lost after that. Then one day, he took off, and we didn't see him for a long time. Dottie was dedicated to the church by that time. She put all her efforts into the children's ministry. When Kenny came back, he was different in a good way. I just wish that he and his momma would reconcile."

"They have," Sameera told him. Mr. Moon's grim expression changed to a slow smile.

"Mr. Moon, you better not be putting the moves on my girl back there," Hippo yelled.

Sameera and Mr. Moon giggled. "Come on, darling. We better get back in there, or I'll have to break his other leg."

They returned, taking their same seats. Hippo was moving from the wheelchair to the styling chair for his turn. Sameera sat next to Mr. Moon, listening to the men talk about the upcoming Superbowl game, but her mind was on what she had just learned about Hippo. She wondered why he hadn't told her about his sister or stepfather. Of course, it was deeply personal. Maybe he wasn't ready to tell her everything. She had questions but decided to wait for him to broach the subject rather than ask him about it.

Chapter Three

~Juan~

Juan Garza was leaving one of his trap houses when his phone rang. He checked the name of the caller. "Hey Tony, what's good?"

"I just left Mr. Moon's shop. Kenny was there."

"And?"

"Nothing. I just thought you would want to know that he's in a wheelchair. Looks like he has a broken leg and was wearing a sling on one arm. Other than that, he looks good."

Juan took a deep breath. "Thanks, Tony. I appreciate the update." He ended the call and stood by his car for a minute, thinking. *Should I drive by the shop?* He shook his head, took out his keys, and got in his car. Juan wanted to see Kenny with his own eyes, but what would that solve? Just because Kenny was at the barbershop didn't mean things had changed.

Juan remembered where he was when he learned about Kenny selling drugs in his neighborhood. Knowing Dottie the way he did, he couldn't believe it was true. He'd been in prison for two years and still had a few to go. His boys were handling his business until he got out. For the most part, things hadn't changed. But a few thought that with him out of the game, they could encroach on his territory. He handed down orders and nipped that shit in the bud real quick.

One day he got a visit from Dottie. He hadn't seen her in a long time. She wasn't the first parent to come directly to him, wanting her son to be pushed out of the drug game. Most sent messages through his boys. He was surprised that she came directly to him. She looked wonderful, but she wasn't there for a reunion. She came to see him because she wanted him to end her son's drug business.

The last thing he'd heard about Kenny was that he wasn't slanging anymore. He was a legitimate businessman who still showed up in the hood but wasn't doing business there anymore. As long as he stayed out of the game, Juan had no reason to fuck with him. What he wanted to know was how he'd gotten injured. Had he gotten into it with someone? If he had, Mr. Moon would know the details. All Juan had to do was ask him about it, but he'd get into that later. He had business to handle first.

~Hippo~

While Malcolm cut his hair, they talked about sports, but Hippo was aware of Sameera's quietness since coming out of the back office with Mr. Moon. She was deep in thought. There was no telling what the old man had said to her while they were alone.

Mr. Moon was worse than any woman. He knew everyone's business and told anyone who came through the barbershop doors. He wasn't malicious about it. Mr. Moon just liked to talk and people listened.

When Malcolm finished his hair, Hippo checked his work in the mirror. "Thanks, man." He paid him and moved back to his wheelchair to leave.

"You are welcome back here anytime you like," Mr. Moon told Sameera as they left.

"Do you still want to see where my mother's house is?"

"Yes."

Hippo gave her directions, pointing out the high school he graduated from when they passed it. His mother lived a few blocks from it. "That's it," he pointed out the white single-story house with the iron fence around it. "She must be at the church. Her car is gone."

"It's a cute house," Sameera said, looking at the two plastic chairs and table on the porch. There were flowers along the walkway. The paint was clean of dirt and looked fresh against the black trim that made it stand out from the other houses. The houses along the street seemed plain and dull in comparison.

Hippo sighed. It was a nice house compared to the others on the block, but that was because his mother worked hard to keep it looking the way it had when his father was alive. She used to keep him and his dad busy pulling weeds up and watering the small yard.

Hippo was enjoying their excursion but was starting to feel the pain of their haircutting adventure. When they left his mother's house, Sameera asked, "Is there anywhere else you'd like to go?"

Shaking his head, he answered, "No. It's time to take a pain pill and rest." He couldn't wait to be completely healed. The throbbing ache that hit him after only doing a little bit of moving to get his hair cut was horrible.

Chapter Five

~Amethyst~

Amethyst put a cup of coffee on her partner's desk before sitting in her chair. They had been sifting through the records from Mr. Bunkers' office for more than a week. Most of it was simple to decipher, but anything about Michelle Leeland was missing.

"The director wants us to debrief him and Kelly Lewis at three."

"Well," Talia said, picking up her drink. "We've got information on all the missing children except for the Leeland baby. Nothing in any of the information I've looked at indicates what happened to Michelle's son."

"I didn't find anything on the kid either. It doesn't make sense that Bunker would keep information about the other children he placed but not the Leeland kid."

"I don't want to be the one to tell this woman that we don't have a clue where her child is," Talia sipped her drink. "Okay, the only reasons that Bunker wouldn't put that information in any of the records he kept would be that the kid died or –"

"Maybe the kid wasn't placed as an adoption," Amethyst interrupted her. "What if he – I don't know – gave the kid to someone else to look after but didn't want a record of it."

"Yeah, but why would he do that?" Talia asked, putting her drink down and sitting up in her chair as she watched the wheels in Am's head turn.

"I don't know, but if there is no record of the adoption, whoever has the child would never have to give the kid back," Amethyst said as a light bulb flashed in her head. "It has to be someone close to him. He gave the kid to someone he knows."

"We need to do a search for anyone close to him who all of a sudden had a kid about the time that Michelle Leeland had her baby."

Amethyst grinned at her partner. That had to be it. The two of them settled in and began searching for relatives or friends with children about four years old. They might get lucky and have the information by the time of the meeting with the director and Ms. Lewis.

~Claudia Bunker~

She stood in the center of her beautiful living room, watching her children playing with their toys. Claudia sighed, closing her eyes. Life wasn't fair. All she wanted was to be a mother, but fate or God didn't believe her worthy of motherhood. She couldn't get pregnant, and she had tried everything possible. They had lost their first adopted child in a horrible accident.

Her desperation was why she had accepted the boy sitting on her floor, making noises like the engine of the car he was playing with. Claudia remembered the night her husband came home with the baby wrapped in someone's dirty tee shirt. The boy couldn't have been more than a few weeks old.

"This baby needs a home," her husband said softly. "Until he can be given back to his mother."

Claudia took the baby from him. "He can stay here with us." They were waiting for a child to adopt, but there was no way of knowing when that would happen. Since both she and her husband were older, it was hard for them. She didn't think they would ever get another child, but they adopted one a few years later.

She couldn't stand the thought of someone coming and taking one of them from her. She would die before giving him up. Kyle was her baby, and she wanted to keep him.

Chapter Six

~Cassidy~

She had been on the job for a week, and so far, Cassidy hadn't seen anything unusual at the bike shop. Goose and his brother Moose were there early and worked late on orders and repairs for their customers. They laughed and teased each other while they worked.

The only other full-time employee was Jasmine, who kept to herself and barely acknowledged Cassidy's presence. She followed the same schedule as the men. Besides saying hey on her way in, Jasmine acted like Cassidy didn't exist.

It was quiet in the front of the store. A few people came in, took a look around, and left. She hadn't sold much merchandise all week, just a jacket to a man who came in to discuss a modification he wanted on his motorcycle.

Goose entered the store from the shop area a little after two in the afternoon. "We're closing up early today," he said, putting out the closed sign and locking the front door.

Goose came in and pulled the drawer from the register. "How did you like your first week on the job?" He stood near her, waiting for her answer.

"Do you want to know the truth?" He nodded.

"I'm bored to death," she said with a giggle.

Goose joined her in laughing. "I told you that."

"I know, but I expected a few more customers to come through."

"Things will get busier in a week or so when we have our bikes in the Cycle Show."

"What's that?"

"It's like a car show, but with motorcycles. They hold it every year. We take our best bikes and show them off. We get a lot of new customers from it, and we auction one off and donate the money to the children's hospital."

"Really?" That surprised her.

"Yeah, wanna see what we're auctioning off this year?"

"Sure," she answered, smiling.

"Come on," he said, moving toward the shop door. Cassidy followed him. "Let me put this in the office," he said, taking the money tray.

When he returned, he led her into a space she hadn't seen. Several motorcycles were lined up in two rows. The last one on the second row was covered. Cassidy took time to look at them all. "These are incredible," she told him, taking in the detailed work and paint jobs. Who does the painting?"

"Moose does the designs, but I do all the painting myself."

They were works of art. When they told her about the customized bikes, she only thought of paint jobs. What she looked at was way bigger than her mind could have ever comprehended. "I've never seen anything like this on the street."

"Most of our customers are from other places, and these are more like showpieces. The owners keep them for shows, but they will occasionally ride them. This is our twenty-twenty-three offering for the auction," Goose said, pulling the drop cloth off.

Cassidy's mouth opened. She moved around the cycle slowly, trying to take in all it was. "Wow."

"We call it Medusa," Goose said with pride.

The motorcycle looked as if the handlebars and the metal workings were snakes coming out of the Goddess's head in the center of the rods running to the front tire.

She started to touch it but stopped. "How much do you guys get for these bikes you auction off?"

"Last year, our Zeus bike went for eighty-five thousand."

"Dollars?" Cassidy said, standing up.

Goose smiled. "Yup."

"That's crazy."

"Hmm, maybe, but we still have a long way to go to take the world's number one most expensive custom bike. Neiman Marcus' Limited Edition Fighter."

"How much is that one?"

"Eleven million."

Cassidy rolled her eyes. "You're telling me someone paid Eleven Million for a motorcycle?"

"Medusa is a bit more practical. I have to take her out for a test run. Would you like to go with me?"

He knew what she was going to say before he finished the question. She was already shaking her head. "No."

"Come on. The first step to getting over your fear is to sit on it. I promise to take it easy."

Cassidy was still shaking her head. She needed to get close to him, and taking this ride would help. "Okay," She conceded.

Chapter Seven

~Juan~

Juan exited his car, crossing the street to get to Mr. Moon's barber shop. He had been sitting in his car for a while, waiting for the customers to clear out. It was closing time, and he wanted to speak to Mr. Moon without an audience.

He stepped inside, locking the door behind himself. Malcolm was sweeping the floor with his back to the door. "We're closed. You'll have to come back on Monday."

"I'm not here for a haircut," Juan said, sitting in one of the chairs near the door. Mr. Moon came out of the office just as his son turned to face Juan.

"Garza," Mr. Moon said, walking towards him. "If you don't want a haircut, what can we do for you?"

"I heard that Kenny was here today."

Malcolm put the broom aside. "So?"

One corner of Juan's mouth rose. "I heard he was in a wheelchair. I want to know why."

Malcom didn't say anything, but Mr. Moon spoke. "Maybe you should speak to him or ask Dottie."

Juan leaned forward, resting his elbows on his knees. "Look, I just want to know what happened to him. That's all."

"Don't you watch the news?"

Juan shook his head. "No. Everything on the news is depressing. I have better things to do with my time. How did Kenny get hurt?"

Malcolm looked at his father, who nodded, letting him know that it was okay to tell Juan. "Kenny's in that biker group, the Road Beasts. They rescued some woman from a trafficking ring, and he got into a fight with one of them and got knocked down some stairs. He broke his collar bone and one of his legs."

"He's going to be fine," Mr. Moon added.

"And this guy that pushed him, who is he?"

"Doesn't matter much," Malcom said, adding, "Kenny's club brother's shot and killed him."

Juan wasn't sure if he was happy about that bit of information. He stood up. "Thank you for telling me." He was grateful for their information but was pissed that he wouldn't get to handle the bastard who hurt his son.

~Sameera~

While Hippo napped, Sameera cleaned the house, did laundry, and called the boys from the club, inviting them over to watch the big game the next day. Then she went grocery shopping to make sure that there was beer and snacks for them.

She was putting away the food when he entered the kitchen. "How are you feeling?"

Hippo stopped by the side of the island. "I had a good nap. "What have you been doing?"

Sameera went through all she had accomplished. Several of The Beasts are coming over to watch the game with you. Right now, I know for sure that Bear,

Carl, Moose, and Goose are coming. Bear is going to contact the others. I hope that I got enough food. I'll make sure everything is ready before I go to Eden's house tomorrow."

Hippo grabbed her hand, kissing it. "Thank you. Without you here, I don't know what I would do."

Her cheeks felt warm, and tingles flowed from where he kissed her hand up her arm and spread through her body. She bit her lip, sliding her hand from his. "I'm sure you would be fine, but I'm glad I could help you through this."

"It's cute that my compliments make you blush," Hippo said softly. He was smiling when she looked at him.

Butterflies danced in her stomach, and warmth spread as he devoured her with his eyes. *How can a few words from him make me feel all gooey inside?* She had never experienced anything like the way he made her feel. Sameera licked her lips and smiled. *Say something, anything.* "What shall we do for dinner tonight?" *I am so lame. I should be flirting with him, but I don't know how. He makes my brain turn to mush when he looks at me like that.*

It took Hippo a minute to answer her question. "I'll take care of dinner tonight. You have done so much for me today that I just want us to Netflix and chill tonight."

"Okay, can we watch Black Panther? I haven't seen it."

The smile she gave him went straight to his heart. He inhaled and sat up straighter in his chair. "We can watch whatever you want."

Chapter Eight

~Goose~

He had no idea how frightened of motorcycles Cherie was until he put the bike in gear and started out of the shop's parking lot. Her arms tightened around his torso so tightly that she felt like a python attacking its prey.

He wouldn't complain because he liked the feel of her arms around him. He went slowly at first, only taking surface streets and maneuvering them away from the shop's area towards the lake in the center of the city.

Goose wanted to get to know her better, the lake was an ideal setting. They would relax and enjoy the ducks and birds, maybe from a picnic table or bench. They could sit and watch the joggers and others walking or riding bicycles along the paths nearby.

It was a beautiful day for their excursion. The sun was out, but it was a bit warmer than usual. They both wore lightweight jackets to keep the cool air at bay during their ride, but once they stopped and got off the motorcycle, they removed them as they walked to a spot not covered by the trees just off the path.

"How do you feel about the ride over here?" Goose asked as they reached an empty table.

Rather than sit on the bench seat, Cherie sat on the tabletop. "It wasn't as bad as I expected." Goose joined her, sitting beside her.

"Good. You held me tightly, but you did well, leaning into the turns."

She pressed her lips together, putting her hand over her heart. "I have a confession to make." She paused, looking at him. "I had my eyes closed the entire time." Goose couldn't stop the bubble of laughter that escaped him. Cherie smacked his arm with the back of her hand. "Don't laugh."

"Sorry. If it will make you feel any better, I did the same thing the first time my dad took me on a ride with him. I was only a kid at the time."

"Is your dad why you got into all this biker business?"

"Yeah. Dad loved motorcycles. He was always in the garage working on one. He'd go to the junkyard and find one that was mangled from an accident, and then he would spend months working on it until it looked and ran as if it were brand new. Then he'd sell it and start on another one."

"Was he a mechanic? Is that what he did for a living?"

"Not officially. He worked in construction. Well, when my mom got onto him and complained that we needed a steady paycheck coming into the house, that is. Cycles were his passion. That could be the reason my mother left him." He was quiet for a moment. It was still painful that she took off, leaving him and his brother when she left their father. He didn't want to get bogged down in his feelings. "What about your family?"

~Cassidy/Cherie~

She hadn't prepared a background story and decided sticking close to the truth would be better.

44

"My mother moved to San Diego for work a few years ago. She's a costume designer."

"Does she design for the movies?"

Cassidy giggled. "That would be cool, but no. She works for a costume shop. They do a lot of work for schools and live theater productions."

"What about your dad?"

"My father died when I was a kid. He worked in law enforcement."

"He was a cop?"

"Yeah," Cassidy answered, trying to keep the sorrow and anger out of her voice.

"Did he die on the job?"

Cassidy didn't miss the softness of his tone when he asked the question. She took a deep breath, turning to face him. "He did. He was killed by some white biker who didn't like being stopped by a black cop."

Goose grabbed her hand, holding it in both of his as he looked into her eyes. "I'm sorry. Is that why you don't like motorcycles?" She didn't say anything. Cassidy closed her eyes and nodded her head. He rubbed her hand with his. "Have you been afraid of them since that happened?"

The contact between their hands was unnerving because she felt a crack in the armor protecting her heart, and excitement flowed into her simultaneously. She slid her hand from his. "Yeah."

"Well, not all bikers are racists, and we're not all bad people, no matter what Hollywood would have you believe."

This was exactly what she wanted. He was opening up about the biker lifestyle. "Are you in a biker gang?"

He laughed again. She glanced at him. He was grinning, and it disarmed her how handsome he looked, with strands of golden hair lifting off his forehead in the breeze. "The Road Beasts aren't a gang. We're a motorcycle club."

"I didn't mean to offend you," she said, looking away from him to the path where joggers and mothers with strollers passed them.

"You didn't. The word gang has a negative connotation. I'll be the first to admit that some clubs fit the word, but The Beasts are different. Each member of my club believes in our vision for it."

"What vision?"

"That we have a purpose of serving our communities using the skills we have. In some way or another, each of us understands the value of people, so we do whatever we can to help our communities. For example, Lion is a doctor, and he's opened a clinic where he can provide medical care without it costing the patients anything."

"How on earth can he do that? You can't get insurance through ObamaCare that cheap."

Goose chuckled. "That's true. It helps that he's got a really smart and wealthy wife. Even without Josie's financial help, he would make it work. Thanks to our club members' varied interests and connections, he gets donations that allow him to do what makes him happy, helping others get well and care for themselves."

Neither of them talked for a while. Cassidy was letting the information Goose had given her soak in.

When she spoke again, it was to ask, "Why do they call him Lion?"

Goose smiled, "Because he's got a great head of hair. Occasionally, he shakes his head. Bear named him that because he looks like a lion when he does it."

"Bear? Do all of you have an animal nickname?" Goose nodded. "What's yours?" She already knew all of their names, but she didn't understand why they had them or how they got them.

"Goose, but I had mine before I joined the club. My brother started calling me that when we were kids. He says it's because of the sound I make when I sleep."

"Is your brother in the club? What's his name?"

"Moose. Bear dubbed him that because it rhymed with mine, because Stephen reminded him of a ten-point buck the way he stands, and because you don't want to piss him off. My brother will come after you head-first if threatened."

"Do you prefer being called by your name or Goose?" Before she left the shop when he hired her, he told her his name, and she had to admit that he looked less like a Cory than Goose.

"People have been calling me Goose for so long that I feel like that is my real name."

"Alright," Cassidy said, getting off the tabletop and standing. "Goose, it is. We should get back. I have some things I need to get done."

He smiled as he got off the table. "Eager for your second ride, huh, or do you want to wrap your arms around me again?"

Cassidy didn't answer, but the warmth in her cheeks gave her away. She was sure that her cheeks were flushed with color. He helped her with her helmet before getting settled on the back. She climbed behind him, holding him tight, but not as tight as before. Cassidy could admit that she liked the feel of his body against hers.

Chapter Nine

~Hippo~

He was excited to see his friends when they arrived at his house on Sunday. Sameera had already left for her girl's date at Eden's house. "Welcome, guys," he said as they entered the house a half hour before the game started. Several of them brought beer, putting it in the fridge and then putting the extras in the ice chest in the living room near the big screen where they were going to watch the game.

Bear and Carl were in the kitchen at the same time, sampling the food. "This is some spread," Bear said, looking the food over.

"You all will have to thank Sameera for it. She put all this together for me."

"How's that going?" Carl asked as he opened a bottle of beer.

Hippo smiled. "Slow and easy." He didn't want to tell them he felt he was failing where Sameera was concerned. The night before, they had chilled in the living room, watching Marvel movies she hadn't seen before. When he thought the moment was right, he tried to kiss her, but Sameera moved away again. He was sure she was into him, and it seemed like she wanted to kiss him too.

She was sitting on his left side, her feet curled under her. Hippo had stretched his arm out along the back of the sofa. Eventually, he slid it around her, pulling her closer to his body. She had snuggled close to him, but when he turned, prepared to lock lips with her, she got up and excused herself to the bathroom.

When she returned, she sat further away from him, and the mood had changed. He'd done something wrong but had no clue what it was.

"Not quite the way I want it to," he admitted.

Some of the other Beasts came into the kitchen. "With a broken body, what do you expect?" Gator asked as he joined them around the counter.

"Trust and believe that you can still do some things. It may cause some pain, but the enjoyable part will more than compensate for it," Rhino said from behind Gator. "I'm speaking from experience on this.

Do you remember the time I broke both my ankles doing that stupid bike stunt on a dare?" They all nodded or said they did. "Well, while I was laid up with metal bolts holding my feet onto my legs, Tavia made me feel like a bucking bronco in a rodeo. She climbed on me and –"

"We get the picture, old man," Cheetah said. "We all love your wife, but we don't want to have that image in our heads."

"Speak for yourself," one of the guys called out from the living room. They all laughed.

"That's not our problem," Hippo said. "We haven't even kissed yet." He didn't intend to talk about his frustrations, but now that he'd opened his mouth, Hippo couldn't stop talking about it.

"Get out of here," Carl said in disbelief.

"No, seriously. She pulls away and closes herself off when I make my move. I'm starting to think that she's not into me. I've never had this problem before."

"Maybe it's not about you," Bear said. "Women are strange creatures. Lica fought me tooth and nail.

The first time I kissed her was in my hammock in the backyard. I had to steal my first kiss."

"Eden put the moves on me. I wasn't prepared for it, and it was the best first kiss I ever had," Carl told them.

"You should just kiss her and let the chips fall where they may," Rhino said.

"No," Hippo shook his head. "She's a lady, and I want to treat her like one. I want her to want my kiss as much as I want to kiss her."

Panther strolled in from the hall. He was the last to arrive. "What's going on in here?"

"Nothing. The game is going to start soon. We should all get settled in the living room," Hippo told them. While he appreciated their input, he didn't want to discuss Sameera with Panther because his friend was interested in her too. The men all moved back into the living room. From then on, they discussed the game and its plays.

Chapter Ten

~Sameera~

Sameera was greeted by Tanya, who answered the door for her when she arrived at Eden's.

"Come in," Tanya said, standing aside.

"Hi, I'm Sameera."

"Pleasure to meet you. I'm Tanya, Eden's cousin."

Sameera followed her into the kitchen. Eden was putting food on the counter. She stopped and came to hug Sameera. "I'm so glad you could come."

"Me too. Can I help with anything?" Sameera asked when Eden let her go.

"No. "You can sit at the counter and tell me what's new and interesting in your life," Eden said, moving back around the counter to finish the potato salad she was making. "Where are you staying?"

Sameera took a seat on a stool at the counter. She was sure that Carl had told her about joining The Beasts. "I'm living with Hippo."

"I had heard that," Eden said before looking over her shoulder at Sameera. "How is that going?" Tanya sat beside Sameera but had to hop up to answer the door when the doorbell sounded.

"Pretty good, I guess." Sameera paused, "Actually, I wanted to talk to you about something."

Eden turned with a large bowl in her hand. She took a spoon from a drawer and began stirring the ingredients. "Okay."

"I'm not sure how to put this, but he's tried to kiss me a few times, and I freeze up and run like a kid in trouble."

Eden scrunched up her face. "Why? You like him, don't you?"

"I like him very much," she said as Cougar entered the room. Sameera was sure that her face was red. She was still embarrassed about finding her and Diego in the laundry room of her house, but she was also embarrassed to talk about her issue. She continued. "I've never been with anyone before. Not even a kiss, and I don't want to mess it up."

"Mess it up?" All three-woman said as if in a chorus.

"You won't mess it up. Trust me," Cougar said, putting a bottle of wine on the counter. "I can see that we need this already. Tanya, get us some glasses, please."

"No fair," Eden whined. "I can't have any."

"Neither can I," Tanya said, pouting. "I'm still breastfeeding the twins."

Cougar humped her shoulders. "Sorry. I didn't think about that."

"No problem," Eden said. "I have some sparkling cyder in the fridge."

Cougar took the glasses from Tanya. "I need a corkscrew." Tanya handed her one. She began opening the bottle. "The best option is to tell him you are inexperienced and need to take things slowly. He will honor that."

While Cougar filled two glasses with wine, Tanya filled two more with cyder for her and Eden. "In the meantime, you need to read a few of my books."

"You're a writer?" Sameera asked.

"Yes, she is," Eden answered. "She writes erotic romances. They will prepare you for – well, you know."

"I have some in the car. I'll get them for you later."

"Thank you," Sameera smiled and sipped from her glass.

"How did you get to be as old as you are without ever kissing anyone?"

"It's probably a cultural thing," Eden said to Tanya, looking at Sameera.

"Partially correct. I was raised in a very traditional Indian home, but I've been on my own for a while now. Honestly, I never met anyone I wanted to kiss or – anything else with."

"But you want to do those things with Hippo?" Tanya asked. Sameera felt her face warm and was sure that they could see the answer written all over her face. "Well, I wish I had told my boyfriend that I was inexperienced before we did it for the first time.

It was awful. We were both inexperienced and no good at communicating."

"Was it that bad?" Cougar asked.

"Child, it was bad. I swear I didn't know it happened because it was over quickly."

"Damn," Eden said, putting the bowl of potato salad down. "My first time was with my best friend. It was nice, but I didn't have an orgasm. I thought something was wrong with me. He was all smiles. I was like, if this is what sex is, I don't want to do it again." The women all laughed. "Don't get me wrong. I liked the sensations I felt, but I didn't have an orgasm until I met Carl, and Lord, have mercy! I was like, this is what it's supposed to feel like."

"What you need to do is masturbate," Tanya said. "You can't expect a man to please you if you don't know how to."

"Mmm, hmm," Cougar said. "Get a couple of different vibrators and figure out what you like."

"Oh, and watch some porn," Tanya said, grinning.

"Porn?" Sameera said, shaking her head. "I couldn't do that. I don't want anyone to know. I could never go buy one."

Tanya smirked. "You don't have to buy anything. Check out Pornhub.com. It's free and very entertaining," she said, licking her lips. "They have everything you could possibly be interested in learning about."

Sameera pressed her lips together before speaking. "I'm also concerned about the size of his penis. Since he's been home he's in sweats, and I can see how large he is."

Tanya started fanning herself. "Honey, I love sweatpants season. Mike knows it too, and he walks through the house with no shirt, rippling muscles and meat just swinging from side to side." Sameera watched as Tanya showed what it looked like by putting her arm in front of her crotch and letting it flop around. Cougar and Eden were having a fit of giggles when the doorbell sounded again.

"Okay, ladies, we need to get it together. That's probably Rabbit or Gazelle. We can't be talking like this in front of the baby Beasts."

They all got quiet as Tanya went to answer the door, but Eden and Cougar snickered from time to time. Sameera couldn't help the smile that was plastered all over her face. Maybe they were right. She should tell Hippo and perhaps even do as Tanya suggested by getting some pleasure tools and checking out the site she mentioned.

Chapter Eleven

~Bunker~

Typically, the game between the Chiefs and the Eagles would have taken over his Sunday activities, but Harrison's mind was on the mess he had made of his life by getting involved with Haji. No matter how he looked at the scenario, he would lose big.

He never expected to have Michelle's son this long, but where else would he be. Harrison was sure that the men he was tied to would never have let Michelle go. They would have killed her or sent her off with the other women to another country, and she would never be heard from again. Kyle was her son, and now that she was free, she should be given a chance to be with him.

He took a deep breath and exhaled slowly. This would cause his wife pain, and that was something he didn't want. Claudia knocked on the door to his office, coming in before he could tell her to. "I was just thinking about you," he told her.

"I hope they were good thoughts," she said, moving closer to his desk.

"I was thinking about you and Kyle. I'm going to see the D.A. soon. Before I do, I need to go over some things with you."

She sat down in the chair across the room. "Okay."

He talked about their finances. "There's more than enough money for you to take care of yourself."

"You sound as if you don't plan on being with us."

"Honey, I'm pretty sure I'm going to prison for my part in all of this. Of course, I'd like to remain a free man, but realistically speaking, that may not be an option. You may have to live frugally, but you will be alright. They'll likely come for Kyle as soon as I tell them the truth about his parentage. You need to prepare yourself to give him up."

"I don't think I can do that."

"You have to. His mother's anguish and suffering, not knowing that her child is safe, healthy, and happy, is too much. We have to give him up."

Claudia got up, crossing the room quickly. She grabbed Harrison's hands, squatting down in front of him. "Don't tell them about Kyle. When you told me who his mother was, you said you never put his name in your records, right?" Harrison nodded. "Then they don't know anything about where he is. You don't have to say anything to them about it."

"Claudia, put yourself in her shoes. If it were your son, what would you want the woman who has loved and cared for him to do? You would want her to return him, wouldn't you?" His wife said nothing. She stood, releasing his hand. "We have to give him up."

"I'm not sure I can," she said, turning and leaving the room. He understood her feelings, but giving up Kyle was what needed to be done.

~Sameera~

By the time she left Eden's house, Sameera felt her head might pop from all she had learned about

63

her new friends. Even though they tried not to, they continued to talk about men and sex.

It was an enlightening conversation. Rabbit was no virgin. While not having a ton of experience, she contributed to their discussion easily. Gazelle, on the other hand, was pretty quiet on the subject. When they asked her why, she explained that she preferred women to men. That took the conversation in a new direction. Tanya was especially interested in Gazelle's sexuality because she wanted to write a same-sex romance.

Several of The Beasts were still there when she returned to Hippo's house. The game wasn't over yet. She caught the score as she pulled into the garage. They were in the fourth quarter of the game. Not wanting to disturb the guys, she eased into the house quietly, went directly to her room, and put the books that Tanya had given her, *His Captive, Under the Moonlight Bridge,* and *Dare Me to Love You,* on the bedside table. She would start reading one of them later.

She took out her phone and went to the site Tanya had given her to buy her first sex toy. She looked through quite a few of the items, not sure what she should try. Tanya suggested not getting any that were meant for penetration. She told Sameera to focus on clitoral stimulation. Sameera still couldn't believe that she was considering buying something like that.

Sameera had just checked out the porn site that was suggested when she heard the front door closing and cars starting. The game must be over. "Sammi?" Hippo called out from the first floor. She put her phone down and left her room.

Chapter Twelve

~Hippo~

By the time she got downstairs, Hippo was in the kitchen, smiling as he waited for her to find him. "Did you just call me Sammi?"

"Yes. If you don't like it, I'll call you Sameera."

"My sister is the only other person who calls me that. It's okay for you to use that name," she smiled at him. "Did you all have a fun time?"

"We did. It was a good game, and as you can see," he said, sweeping his hand over the counter. "The guys cleaned up before leaving. They said to thank you for all the food. Did you have fun with the girls?"

She smiled again. "I did. It was an interesting afternoon."

"What did you do?"

"We gossiped about old boyfriends, husbands, and things like that."

"You told them about your previous relationships?"

"Me?" She asked, putting her hand on her chest as she came further into the kitchen. "No."

"Why not?"

"Because I've never had one."

His eyes bugged out a bit. "You've never had a boyfriend before?"

"No. I'm a virgin in all aspects of male-female relationships."

Hippo stared at her, his face blank of expression until he slowly began a smile that turned into a full grin. "You're not joking, are you?"

"No."

He cocked his head to one side. "Is that why you won't kiss me?" She nodded slowly. "But you do want to kiss me, right?"

He knew he sounded like an inexperienced teen boy, but that's how he felt. He was used to being the one who pushed to get the relationship to move forward, but with Sameera, he would take a step back and let her do the chasing.

Sameera nodded her head. "I do, but I'm scared I'll do it wrong, and you'll never want to do it again."

"Not possible," Hippo said sincerely. The fact that Sameera was completely untouched turned him on in a big way. "Don't worry about that. I'll always want to kiss you."

Sameera's cheeks bloomed with color. "Are you willing to go slow for me, take it at a leisurely pace?" He nodded, smiling. "Good." She drummed her fingers on the counter. "Since I don't have to clean up the house, I'm going to take a bubble bath and read a book. Are you good? Do you want anything?"

He wanted her, but he could wait now that it was clear that she wanted him. "I'm good," he told her as flashes of her relaxing in the deep soaker tub in his bathroom filled his mind. *Down boy,* he mentally told his dick, which might pop out of his pants and scare her half to death at any moment. *We'll get to that when she's ready.*

Sameera surprised him by coming to where he sat to kiss his cheek. "Good night, Kenny," she told him, smiling brightly as she left the room.

His heart was pounding heavily, and his tummy was alive with thousands of butterfly wings fluttering.

Chapter Thirteen

~Sameera~

After her bath, Sameera stood at the foot of the bed, holding her towel. Since sleeping in his bed, she had gotten used to Hippo's scent left on his sheets and pillows, but she had done the laundry and changed the linens. It no longer smelled like him. All she could smell was the Downy fabric softener.

Smiling to herself as an idea came to her, Sameera put the towel back in the bathroom before going to the drawer where she'd found his boxer briefs and took out a pair. Then she moved to the drawer with tee shirts and removed one, sniffing it. *Yup, smells good.* She put them on quickly before grabbing her brush and phone. She got comfortable on the bed and brushed her hair to stimulate her scalp as she did every night, as her mother had taught her.

When she was finished, she dialed her sister's number.

"Hey, Sammi," her sister said when she answered.

"What's wrong?" Sameera asked. She knew her sister well enough to know that her tone was off.

"What makes you think something is wrong?"

"I know you better than anyone else in this world. What's wrong?"

"Nothing. I was just thinking about you, and I miss you. That's all."

Sameera didn't believe that nothing was wrong. "If you miss me, why don't you come for a visit. Alone," she added. Sameera didn't want her fiancé to tag along.

"I'd like that, but I don't think mom and dad will allow it."

"Then don't tell them. Write them a note, and come to visit. They'll see it after you leave, and then there is nothing they can do until you return." Sameera didn't believe that the problem was just about her parents. She was sure it also had to do with her future husband.

"I don't know," Haimari said hesitantly.

71

"You don't have to pack clothes or anything. Get your purse and go to the airport. I'll buy you a ticket. All you have to do is get on the plane."

There was a long pause. Sameera expected Haimari to tell her no, but to her surprise and delight, Haimari agreed. "Okay. When should I leave?"

"Right now. Call me when you get to the airport."

"Okay. I love you, Sammi."

"I know. I love you too." As the call ended, Sameera took a deep breath, letting it out. She realized she hadn't talked to Hippo about it, but she was sure he wouldn't mind her sister staying there for a few days.

She grabbed her phone and went down to talk to him about it. The door to his room was closed. She knocked and waited for him to answer.

"Come in," he called out.

~Hippo~

Thankfully, he hadn't removed his sweatpants yet. Hippo had gotten into the habit of getting naked after being sure that Sameera was not coming back downstairs. He started grinning like a crazy man when he realized Sameera was wearing his clothes, especially his underwear.

"Did you come to kiss me goodnight?" He asked, playfully wiggling his eyebrows up and down.

She was quiet for a second or two. "I will kiss you if you say yes to what I'm about to ask you."

She was looking down and away from him. Her voice was soft, and she sounded unsure of herself.

While Hippo was happy that she offered a kiss, he didn't want it this way. He moved his chair closer, forcing her to look at his face.

"I will give you whatever you want, and you don't have to use yourself as collateral, okay?"

She smiled, meeting his eyes. "My sister needs a break from our parents and her fiancé. Is it okay if she comes here for a few days or so?"

73

The corner of his mouth went up. She sounded like a child asking for dessert before dinner had been served, anticipating that she wouldn't get what she wanted.

"Of course, she can come," he said, grabbing her hand. The smile she gave him sent the butterflies dancing inside him.

"Thank you," she said with a sigh. "She won't be any trouble. She can sleep with me, and I'll take her with me during the day, so you won't have to be bothered."

"Now, I'm jealous," Hippo said, winking at her. "She'll get more time with you than I do. When will she be here?"

"Tonight or in the morning. I wanted to get your permission before I bought her ticket."

"This is your home. You don't need my permission to invite your family here for future reference, okay?" She smiled again, and for a second, he couldn't breathe.

"Thanks, Kenny." Sameera bent over and kissed his cheek before leaving him. "Goodnight," she called out from down the hall.

Chapter Fourteen

~Sameera~

For a fraction of a second, Sameera freaked out at the warmth coming from behind her. Then she remembered that it was Haimari sleeping in the bed with her. Sameera grabbed her phone from the bedside table to check the time.

She turned off the alarm that would sound in a few minutes. Slipping out of bed, she glanced at her sister. Haimari opened her eyes. She stretched, rolling onto her back. "Morning."

"I have to get going in a little while. You can stay and sleep if you want to," Sameera said, moving around the room to get her clothes.

"Can I go with you?" Haimari asked, sitting up.

"Sure," Sameera said, opening the door to the bathroom. "We need to leave in about forty-five minutes, and I have to make something for Kenny to have for breakfast."

Haimari got out of bed, pushing the hair away from her face. "When will I get to meet your friend?"

"Depends whether he's up or not," Sameera told her as she closed the door, adding. "Find something comfy to put on from the drawers on the left side of the dresser."

While she was thrilled that her sister had come to visit. Haimari still hadn't told Sameera why she needed to escape from her fiancé and their parents, but she would talk about it when she was ready. In the meantime, Sameera would make sure that her sister enjoyed herself.

Sameera would also tell her sister for the first time what she had been doing with her life. She was certain that Haimari would think she was crazy for becoming a thief and joining a motorcycle club.

After finishing in the bathroom, she went back into the bedroom. Hairmari was dressed in a pair of Sameera's leggings and a hoodie. "I'll be in the kitchen. I put a toothbrush on the counter for you."

Haimari hugged her, kissing her cheek. "Thank you for helping me get a break from everything."

Sameera sighed at the sad sound of her voice. "No problem." Haimari went into the bathroom, and Sameera grabbed her phone and keys before going to the kitchen.

She was surprised to find Kenny standing over the stove and, cooking. "What are you doing?"

"Making you and your sister breakfast," he said as he turned off the burner. "I made scrambled eggs and toast."

"No bacon?" Sameera grinned, walking towards him.

"I was planning to, but I don't think there is enough for the three of us."

"I'll stop by the store on the way home and get some. Is there anything else I need to get?"

"I don't think so," he replied, using the spatula to put eggs on the plates lined up on the counter.

A few minutes later, her sister joined them. "Kenny, this is Haimari," Sameera introduced them.

Haimari smiled. "Hi, Kenny."

"Wow, you're as pretty as your sister," Hippo said when he turned to get a look at her.

Haimari blushed, "Thank you."

"Let me get those," Sameera said, moving closer to him. She reached over his wheelchair, took a plate, and handed it to Haimari. "Kenny made us breakfast."

"That was nice of you," Haimari said as she took the plate from her sister.

"You get off that leg," Sameera fussed as she angled Hippo's chair so he could sit in it. "Show Haimari to the dining room, and I'll get our plates."

~Hippo~

He wasn't surprised by how good-looking Haimari was. The two looked similar, with large almond-shaped eyes surrounded by long dark lashes. Their noses were nearly identical, but Haimari's was slightly broader and less upturned. They both had full lips, and their bodies were about the same. Haimari was taller, though.

They were quiet at the table, focusing on their meal rather than talking. He noticed that Haimari glanced at him frequently. When their eyes met, she smiled. "How did you two meet?" She asked between bites.

Since Sameera rarely talked about her family with him, Hippo wasn't sure what Haimari knew about him. He chose to let Sameera answer the question.

Sameera looked at Hippo and then faced her sister. "We met when I was helping plan a wedding for one of his friends."

So, she doesn't know the truth. Hippo said nothing. Her answer was the truth. *Well, that is partially.*

"Is that what you do, plan weddings?" Haimari was smiling when she said it.

"Not exactly. I'll tell you on the way to the gym," Sameera said, glancing at Hippo as if waiting for him to out her.

Hippo kept his mouth shut. It wasn't any of his business. If Sameera wanted to keep secrets, he wouldn't get involved, but he would tell her what he thought when he got to speak to her alone.

When they finished eating, Sameera and her sister took the dishes back into the kitchen. Hippo was returning to his room when Sameera said, "We should be back around four. Call me if you need anything."

"Have a good day," Hippo said as he rolled into his room.

Chapter Fifteen

~Kelly~

"What do you mean he's dead?" Kelly said into the phone. Mondays were always awful, but this one started out worse than the others. The minute she sat in her plush leather chair, she got a call informing her that one of the men trafficking the women that The Beasts freed had been found hanging in his cell. "I want the details about this. Who was the last person to see him alive? Did anyone see something?" She listened to the answers and was not pleased. They believed that it was suicide, but Kelly's instinct told her that the man had been killed. By who, she had no idea. "Thanks, but I want a detailed report and the other men isolated from the rest of the population. Someone might be getting rid of a trail that will lead to the people in charge." She hung up the phone and sat back in her chair, closing her eyes and blowing air from her mouth.

A million things raced through her mind. The police didn't seem to think that Roger Stanton had been murdered. It looked like suicide, and they were putting it down as that. Kelly wasn't so sure that it was that simple. Stanton could have had valuable information about the trafficking ring. So could the other men. That's why she wanted them secluded from the rest of the prisoners. Based on the data that the FBI had from Bunker's office, he was her next best witness. She needed to get to him before someone else did.

She didn't want to put him in lock up for fear that he'd be found hanging in his cell like Stanton. There was only one thing she could think of doing. Kelly picked up her cell phone, found the person she wanted, and hit send.

The phone rang a few times before being answered. "Well, well, well. This is a surprise."

"I need a favor," Kelly said, ignoring him.

"And you called me of all people?"

Kelly had expected her father to give her a hard time, but she also knew he would do what she wanted. "You said to call you if I needed help with anything. I need your help, and I'll pay you."

Her father sighed heavily. "What do you need me to do?"

"I'm working a case, and a guy that may have information could be in danger. I need someone to look after him. I'll pay you five hundred to get him and keep him somewhere no one knows until I can get this sorted out." She hoped that the money would help him agree to her request.

"Who is this guy, and how long will I have to play bodyguard?"

Kelly gave him the details, including Bunker's office address. "He knows nothing about me and why I want to keep him safe."

"So, you want me to kidnap him?"

"That's not what I'm saying. Once you explain who I am and that one of the men he was working with died while locked up, I think he'll go willingly."

"Okay."

"Call me when you get him," she said before ending the call. He could be relied on, and the only way that he could be tied to her was someone already knew about their connection. Kelly grew up believing that her father was the man who raised her. It wasn't until her mother died that she discovered he was her real dad.

He had come to the funeral. He watched her from a distance and spoke with her mother's husband, the man Kelly believed to be her father. After he left, she asked her father, Joseph, about the man. He told her the truth. She was shocked and not sure what to think.

When she finally decided to meet him, she had an investigator track him down. He explained why everyone had lied to her. He gave her his number before she left and told her to call him if she ever needed anything. Now she had. She hoped that it was the right thing to do.

Chapter Sixteen

~Hippo~

After Sameera and her sister left, Hippo got his laptop out and reviewed the list of emails in his inbox. Most were junk mail that he deleted quickly. There were a few from Tiffany with information about his CBD stores.

He read and replied to most. It looked like everything was well. He knew it had been a great idea to hire his cousin after she finished college. They were on track to open a new location in a few months. First, he wanted Panther to examine his finances and ensure nothing seemed problematic. They could start looking at sites in a month or two if everything lined up correctly.

The doorbell rang just as he closed the lid on his computer. Hippo grabbed his phone and pulled up the app for his doorbell. His mother was standing there, waving at the camera. He unlocked the door from the phone and held down the mic button. "It's open."

It only took his mother a few minutes to get to his room. "I hope you don't mind me just stopping by," she said as she entered the room.

"I'm surprised to see you."

"Well, normally I'd be at the church working, but we had a pipe burst, and water was everywhere. Pastor Henley gave me the day off while he tries to get it fixed. With our budget being what it is, we may have to shut the church down for a while."

"Really?"

His mother sighed as she sat down in the chair near him. "Yeah. Things haven't been great for a while. Tithes and donations are down. The paster can barely pay the cleaning lady and me. It won't be long before the church closes at the rate we're going."

Hippo had never been big on religion, but he knew that his mother's church did a lot of good in the community. "Is the pastor there right now?"

"Yeah. He's calling around to see if he can find a plumber to come take a look at the damage. More than likely, we won't be able to pay for the work they'd have to do."

Hippo grabbed his phone and went through his contacts. He dialed Carl's number and waited for him to answer. "Hey, Hippo," Carl said. "How are you feeling?"

"I'm good, but I need help with something. The church on Second Avenue, Calvary Baptist, had a pipe burst. They could use some help fixing the problem. Can you send someone over there to check it out?"

"Yeah, I can send Cheetah and Gator. They're not doing any work for Bear and me this week. I'll call Bull too. He can check the electrical."

"Their budget will be an issue. I'll cover the cost of any work that needs to be done. Tell the pastor that my mother Dorothea sent them."

"Will do," Carl said, hanging up.

"You didn't have to do that," his mother said, sounding like she might cry.

"Mom, don't cry."

"I can't help it," she said, sniffing and wiping her eyes. "This means more than you know."

Hippo understood what the church meant to her. He could help, and he knew that the club would too. "Mom, this is the kind of thing that my club does. We help those we can. Fixing the church is right up their alley. Carl and Bear run a construction business, and we have members like Cheetah and Gator who are licensed plumbers."

"I had no idea. I just always thought they were a bunch of miscreants."

Hippo snickered. "They are, but they have big hearts too."

"Maybe you should tell me more about your friends." He smiled, happy that maybe he could display them in a good light, that she would see and understand that people he considered family weren't bad.

Chapter Seventeen

~Sameera~

They were getting close to the gym, and
Sameera hadn't told her sister what she did for a
living. She was hoping that Haimari would forget
about it.

"Tell me what you do for a living if you're not a
wedding planner."

Sameera gripped the steering wheel a bit tighter.
"I'm a burglar." She looked at her sister from the
corner of her eyes.

"If you don't want to tell me, just say so. There's
no need to lie."

They stopped at a light. Sameera turned to look
into her sister's eyes. "I'm a thief. That's what I've
been doing since I ran off. I started out picking
pockets when we were kids. I thought I was pretty
good at it until this guy spotted me in Miami. I was
working the beach." She turned back to traffic. She
didn't see the point of telling her about how she met

Panther. "That's where I was when the investigators that Mom and Dad hired found me. When I took off again, I knew I could never go back home after embarrassing them the way I did, running out on my wedding. So, I found a more lucrative way to support myself. I learned how to get into places that had valuable stuff. I'd take what I needed and then sell it."

"This doesn't make any sense. You have money sitting in an account –"

"That is not my money. It's their money – our parents. I couldn't take from them after I let them down. That's why I've never used it. I had to be independent and make my own way in the world. I did it by stealing things." She half smiled. "I'm good at it, but it caught up to me last year when I stole something from a drug lord's house. His people found me, and he gave me a choice, I could work for him or die. He had me sitting around his house until the day he sent me here, to Dallas, with the order to steal a woman's child."

"What?" You didn't, did you?"

"No." Sameera shook her head as she turned into the gym's parking lot. "I never intended to do it. When I got the chance, I told Eden about it, betraying him – and gaining a new family. He ordered a hit on Eden's husband and me. Fortunately, his hitmen failed, and The Beasts took him out."

Haimari was staring at her. "They killed him?" Sameera nodded. "Beasts? What do you mean by that?"

Sameer turned the car off and explained who the Road Beasts' were and how she met Hippo. "Now, I'm joining their motorcycle club to use my skills for something good. They help the people of this city." She told Haimari about the saved women and how she was helping them locate the children. "This is where I belong. This is what I was meant to do." Haimari just stared at her for a minute. "Say something, anything."

Haimari grabbed her hand. "You have to give me a minute. That's a lot to take in."

"I have to get in there. Mike is very serious about punctuality," Sameera said, removing her seatbelt and opening her door.

Haimari got out of the car, looking over the roof. She asked, "Who is Mike?"

"Mike is a security specialist who is training me in self-defense. I'm also in gun training."

"You've changed a lot from the bratty kid that I knew."

Sameera didn't say anything, but her sister was smiling. Everything would be okay between them.

~Panther~

Getting out of his car, Panther grabbed his leather satchel and put the strap over his head. He ensured his white button-down was smooth beneath the belt across his chest. He closed the door to his car, sliding on his aviator sunglasses. He should have put his jacket on. It was a cool day, but Mike wouldn't care if he looked like a businessman, unlike the client he had just left.

He didn't need sunglasses to walk from his car to Mike's Gym entrance, but the sun was shining. He crossed the parking lot and entered. During the day, the area near the entry was empty unless Mike taught a self-defense class. It wasn't empty today.

Mike was working with Sameera, who was fending Mike off in a mock attack. She dropped to the floor, rolling away from him, but Mike kept coming at her until she got hold of his hand and twisted him around, flipping him onto his back.

"Good," Mike said, standing up. "That was good. You caught me by surprise. At that moment, you can either run or continue your assault against your attacker if you feel the need to." Mike hopped up from the floor, looking behind Sameera. Panther's eyes followed, and he was struck dumb by the woman sitting on the floor watching. She looked a lot like Sameera. "You want to give it a try?" Mike asked the woman.

"I couldn't do anything like that," she said, shaking her head.

Panther didn't hear the rest of the conversation. He watched as the woman got up. She was taller than Sameera, and her body was a bit curvier. She was strikingly beautiful. He watched as Mike showed her a few moves and had her practice them. Panther took off his sunglasses just as Mike noticed him. "Excuse me. Practice with your sister while I talk to Panther," Mike said, moving away from the women. Both of them glanced in his direction. He smiled as he got a look at the woman's face. ***Stunning.***

"Hey," Mike said as he approached.

"I didn't mean to interrupt. My last meeting ended early, so I came straight here instead of going back to my office."

"No problem. Let's get you the paperwork you need to get started." When he didn't move, Mike looked back at the women. "Which one has your attention?"

Panther snapped his head around to Mike. "Both, but who is that?"

"Sameera's sister, Haimari. She's visiting for a while." Mike told him as they walked to his office.

Chapter Eighteen

~Sameera~

When Mike and Panther were out of sight, Haimari whispered, "Who was that guy? Did Mike call him Panther?"

Sameera smiled. "Yes, Panther is his club name. He's one of The Beasts."

"He doesn't look like he'd be in this club, and what's with the animal names? You called Kenny Hippo last night when you told me who the house belonged to."

"All the club members have animal names, and as for how he looks, you should see him in his casual clothes."

Haimari shook her head. "No wonder you wanted to come back to Dallas. You're surrounded by hot guys."

Sameera couldn't help the laugh that bubbled up and out of her. "I'm not here because of the men." Haimari tilted her head to one side, pursing her lips.

"Okay," Sameera said, humping her shoulders. "I came back for one in particular."

"I knew it. So, something is going on with you and Kenny."

It wasn't a question, but Sameera treated it like it was. "Yes. We like each other and are getting better acquainted."

"I want details right now."

"Alright," Sameera sat on the floor and waited for her sister to join her. "Most of the club members are men. Mike's brother, Carl, was the leader. He's married to Eden, the woman whose baby I was supposed to kidnap. Now, Cougar was elected to lead when Carl stepped down. I was staying with her, but I walked in on her and her man having sex and realized that I couldn't continue living there. Hippo had been injured when they saved all these women from traffickers, and he told me I could stay with him."

"What's the deal with this Panther guy? He was staring at you."

"He likes me too, but I shut him down because Kenny makes the butterflies explode in my belly every time I see him."

"Are all the men in the club super sexy?"

Sameera sighed, "Depends on what you define as sexy, but nearly all of them are."

"This visit might be more worth it than I thought."

"You're engaged. Don't forget that."

Haimari made a face. "You were right. I don't love Raja, and I don't want to marry him. I've been thinking about it since you left."

"Is that why you wanted to come here?"

"I left mom and dad a note, telling them I would call them in a few days."

"What about Raja?"

"They'll tell him that it's over."

Sameera flopped back, lying on her back. This was the worst thing that could have happened. Now, not only had she run out on her arranged marriage, but so had her sister.

Chapter Nineteen

~Panther~

It didn't take Mike long to gather the information Panther needed to do the taxes for the gym. Panther wanted to leave the office and learn more about Sameera's sister. He put the information that Mike gave him into his satchel, turning to leave when Mike's office phone rang.

Panther waved and returned to where the women were sitting on the floor. He stopped close to them, squatting to get closer to their level.

"Hello, ladies."

"Hi. Panther. This is my sister Haimari."

Panther held out his hand to Sameera's sister. "My government name is Quincy Carter. It's a pleasure to meet you, Haimari."

She looked him in the eye before taking his hand. "It's nice to meet you too."

Haimari let his hand go. "Sameera never mentioned that she had a sister. How long are you going to be in town?" ***Please say you'll be here for a while.***

"I'm not sure."

"At least through the end of the week," Sameera supplied.

Panther smiled, keeping his attention on Haimari. "Do you have plans for Wednesday night?"

"Valentine's day?" Haimari questioned. "Are you asking me on a date?"

His smile turned into a full grin. He didn't want to be aggressive about it, but that's exactly what he was doing. "Well, I figured that Sameera and Hippo probably have plans. I thought that we could have dinner or something. You know, give them the night to themselves."

Haimari turned to her sister. "I had forgotten all about the holiday coming up. Do you have plans?"

"Yeah, I have something in mind."

Haimari's eyes flicked back to Panther. "Well, in that case, I accept your invitation."

"Great. I assume you are staying at Hippo's. I will pick you up at seven," Panther said, standing up again. He looked at his watch. "I have to get back to work. I have a client meeting in half an hour. I look forward to seeing you in a few days."

"Me too," Hairmari told him with a soft smile.

That smile is going to be the end of me. "Bye, ladies," he said, leaving them.

~Sameera~

Haimari watched him walk away. When he went out the door, Haimari turned back to Sameera, who had one eyebrow raised.

"What?" Haimari asked.

"You're engaged."

"Technically."

"There is no 'technically' about it. Until you tell Raja it's off, you are engaged."

"So, then, are you still engaged to Amir?"

Sameera rolled her eyes. "No."

"Then neither am I. Besides, it's just dinner, and he's only taking me out to give you and your man some alone time on the most romantic day of the year."

"Yeah, right." Sameera was inexperienced but not stupid. The sparks flying between her sister and Panther were glaringly obvious. Even though he admitted to being interested in Sameera, Panther had never looked at her like he looked at Haimari. *Am I objecting to this date because I'm jealous? No, it can't be that. Panther is handsome and interesting, but I don't like him that way. I'm just looking out for my sister. That's all.*

Chapter Twenty

~Bunker~

It was nearly lunchtime when Harrison's secretary buzzed him. He assumed she was checking to see if it was okay for her to take her break. "Yes," he said, hitting the speaker button on the office phone.

"There's a man here to see you, and he refuses to give me his name."

Harrison's heart rate increased dramatically. *I thought I would have more time before the cops came for me. Then again, it might not be the cops. It could be Haji's people coming to make sure that I can't speak to the police.*

"Mr. Bunker?" His secretary asked to see if he was still on the line.

"Send him in," Harrison told her. He stood up, putting his jacket on. *Calm down. It's probably nothing, but why wouldn't he give Margret his name if that were the case?*

The door to his office opened as he moved around the desk. "Are you Harrison Bunker?" The man asked as Margret stood in the doorway.

"You can go to lunch now, Margret."

She left, leaving him alone with this guy. He turned his attention to the man standing between him and the door. "I am. Who's asking? My secretary said that you wouldn't give her your name?" Harrison looked the man over. He was dressed casually in jeans and a plain tee shirt under his denim jacket. He was tall and muscular with medium-toned skin, dark hair, and eyes. He could be one of Haji's men, but he sounded American when he spoke.

"Yeah, I thought it would be best if she didn't know my name if someone came here looking for you."

Harrison's brow furrowed. "What do you mean?"

"The D.A. Kelly Lewis asked me to come to get you. She believes that your life is in danger. I'm to take you somewhere and keep you safe."

"I don't understand what's going on?" He hadn't contacted her office yet. How would she know about his involvement? He closed his eyes. *One of the men they arrested must have talked. Fuck, I am in danger.*

"Look, I don't know the details. I was asked to come to get you, and that's what I'm doing."

What if this is some kind of trick? "How do I know that you are a cop? You could be the one who is going to kill me."

"I'm not a cop. Kelly is my daughter. Feel free to call her to verify this, but whatever you are going to do, you need to do it so we can get going."

Harrison watched the guy for a second or two, trying to determine his trustworthiness. "Give me a second," he said, pulling out his cell phone. He Googled the Dallas District Attorney's office and dialed the number he found. He asked for Kelly Lewis and was transferred.

"This is Kelly Lewis," a woman said.

"Ms. Lewis, my name is Harrison Bunker –"

The woman interrupted him. "Mr. Bunker, I'm glad to hear your voice. Listen carefully. I'm sending someone to get you. His name is Juan Garza. He's my father."

"He's here now," Harrison said.

"May I speak with him?" Harrison handed the man the phone. He listened to Mr. Garza's side of the conversation. It was brief. The man didn't say much before he handed the phone back to him.

"I'm here."

"Mr. Bunker, I'll explain everything to you in person, but I need you to trust me and go with my father."

"I have a family. I can't just disappear." There was a short silence from the other end of the call.

"I'll arrange to have your family picked up."

"I need to speak to Claudia myself. I need to tell her that someone is coming for her."

"Alright, call her now, but make sure she understands she can't tell anyone I'm putting you and them in protective custody. Do you understand?"

"Yes."

"Good. I'll send someone to your house in the next hour. Mr. Bunker, we have a lot to talk about. I hope that you are willing to cooperate."

"I am, but you have to keep my family safe."

"I'll do my part if you do yours."

When she ended the call, Harrison put the phone in his pocket. Moving around his desk, he said. "Give me just a minute. I need to get a few things to take with me."

He also wanted to write a note to Margret that he would be away from the office for a while and that she could take some time off. He didn't want her to be there if anyone came looking for him.

Once he and Mr. Garza were in his car, Harrison dialed his wife's number. "Hello?"

"Claudia, honey, I need you to listen carefully. I spoke with the D.A. I don't have all the details of why, but I trust her. She's sending someone to the house to get you and the boys. You can't tell anyone what's happening, and you must be ready in the next forty minutes or so. Do you understand what I'm saying to you?"

"Yes, what about you?"

"She sent someone she trusts to get me. I've already left the office and told Margret to take a few days off. I'll see you soon."

"Okay," she said just before he hit the end button.

Everything is going to be okay.

Chapter Twenty-One

~Hippo~

Dottie spent the morning wiping down furniture, though it was already clean. It was just something she had always done. She started in Hippo's room, wiping invisible dust and dirt from his bedside table, then his dresser. Before he knew it, she had disappeared into the rest of the house.

She left him alone for a while. When she returned to the room, he said, "Mom, you don't have to do that."

She smiled. "I can't help it. I like to keep busy. I'd go home, but there is nothing for me to do there."

Hippo believed her because she had always been a very neat person. Cleaning was one of the first things she taught him and his sister to do. He sighed as he thought about his sister. After all this time, he still hadn't gotten over what had happened to her.

"What's wrong?" His mother asked him as she sat down in the chair near him.

He didn't want to talk to her about it. In his heart, he knew that she blamed him for Marilynn's disappearance. She wouldn't have gotten taken if he had not been hanging out trying to make money at the park. He was supposed to walk with her from school, but he was being irresponsible. "Nothing, just thinking about some things."

"Okay. Why don't you tell me how things are going between you and Sameera?"

Hippo was grinning the moment his mother said her name. "There's not much to tell. She's been busy with her training. We don't get to spend much time together. Now that her sister is here, I'm afraid she won't have time for me."

His mother's hand flapped as she said, "Honey, please. She'll make time for you. She likes you a lot."

His smile grew bigger. "What makes you think that?"

"If she didn't have feelings for you, she wouldn't have told me the truth about your beasty friends. She did that because she wanted us to get past our issues and have some sort of relationship.

She would have kept her mouth shut like Bailey if she didn't care."

His smile dropped at the mention of his ex. "Is that why you don't like her?"

His mother shook her head. "That's a part of it. I always felt that she didn't love you the way you seemed to love her. The few times that I saw you two together, your relationship seemed very one-sided. I'm just glad that it's behind you. Now, you can focus on this new relationship. I think Sameera is a great catch for you."

"You barely know her."

"That may be the case, but I have developed good instincts about people and see potential in her. She's young and focused. The two of you can build a great life together. You can have children with her."

Hippo looked at her. "Is that another reason you didn't like Bailey, because she was too old to have children?"

"The thought did cross my mind, and for the record, I didn't – I don't dislike her. I just knew she

111

wasn't the one for you. Have you told Sameera about your relationship with Bailey yet?"

"No, I haven't."

"You should. Couples with secrets don't fare well when those bones start popping out of the closet."

"Are you telling me that you and dad never had any secrets from each other?"

"No. I told him everything about my past when I met him because I didn't want it to mess up what we could have together."

"Everyone has secrets," Hippo said, leaning back against the pillow. "Everyone."

His mother was quiet for a minute. "That's true. Everyone has something that they don't want to share with the person they love, but you have to weigh the information and determine if it is worth the consequences that will come with the secret-spilling out later. As much as I believe in total honesty in most relationships, I also think some secrets are better if kept that way."

She contradicted herself, but Hippo believed he understood what she was getting at. "I don't plan to keep it a secret from her. I'm just not ready to tell her yet."

"All I'm saying is to be careful how long you wait to tell her. Sometimes when you hold a secret for a long time, it becomes impossible to tell someone the truth."

Hippo turned his head to see her face. It sounded like his mother did have secrets, and she might regret not telling the truth. The doorbell rang, interrupting them. His mother got up to answer it.

When she came back into the room, she was accompanied by Gator.

"Hey," Hippo greeted him. "What are you doing here?"

"I came to give you an update. I know I could have called, but I wanted to check on you too."

"Gator, this is my mother."

"It's a pleasure to meet you, Mrs. Thompson," Gator said with a warm smile.

"Can I get you anything?" Hippo's mother asked.

"No, thank you. Okay, the damage isn't as bad as I thought. Cheetah is going to pick up what we need from Home Depot. I got the water turned off, and once we get all the water sucked out of there, it won't take but a few days to fix the issue. The church will need to replace the carpet, and that's about it."

"That's good news," Hippo's mother said, raising her hands. "Thank you, Jesus."

"I can write you a check," Hippo told him, moving to get out of bed.

"Oh, no. When Carl asked me to come over, he said this was on him and Bear. So, your money is no good."

"Are you sure? I told him that I would cover the cost of the repairs."

"You two can hash it out, but I don't think you will win this one. He was pretty clear about his intention to pay for it."

Hippo's phone chirped, but Tiffany called out from the hall before he could pick it up. "Kenny, it's

Tiff." She entered the room. She stopped and smiled at everyone. "Are you having a party and didn't invite me?"

"No, we're just taking care of some business," he told her. "Gator, this is my cousin, Tiffany."

"Gator? You must be in his club," she said, holding out her hand to him. Gator didn't shake it. He took hold and lifted it to his lips, brushing them lightly over the back. A soft giggle escaped her before she pulled out of his grasp. "Well, that was different."

Gator grinned. "Well, it isn't every day that I meet a goddess in the flesh."

Hippo rolled his eyes. "Oh, God." It was the first time he'd actually seen a woman swoon.

"Shut up, bucket head. Let the man worship me as I deserve to be," Tiffany said, still looking at Gator.

"Did you bring what I asked for?" Hippo asked his cousin.

"Yeah," she said, looking away from his club brother. She took a file folder from her bag and handed it to Hippo. "If your accountant needs anything else, let me know." She glanced at Gator again. "As much as I want to stick around, I have to get back to work."

"I'll walk out with you," Gator said, then he dipped his head to Hippo's mother. "Don't worry about the church. It will be as good as new when we finish everything."

Hippo was shaking his head as they left. His mother followed them down the hall, most likely to lock the door, but Hippo also thought she was just nosey and wanted to see if they exchanged numbers. Hippo wasn't sure who would get the worst of it if they hooked up. Gator was a ladies' man who was used to dating around, and Tiffany was the kind of woman who always had a few guys hanging around, waiting for the chance to get in where they fit in.

Chapter Twenty-Two

~Gator~

As they went through the door, Gator said, "So, you work for Hippo?"

Tiffany used her key fob to unlock her car. "Yes. I manage his CBD stores."

"Stores? I knew he had one, but he has more?" He put his hand on her car, effectively stopping her from getting in it.

She pressed her lips together and smiled, turning to face him. "Look, Gator," she said, looking him in the eye. "It's cute what you're doing, but I don't date white guys."

"Why not? Are you prejudiced?"

Tiffany made a face, raising one eyebrow and twisting her mouth to one side. "Yeah, I am."

Gator grinned at her. "I don't believe you. You may not have ever dated a colorless man, but I'm interested in being friends at the very least."

"Friends?" Tiffany questioned him. "Tell the truth and shame the devil," she said, shaking her head.

"Okay. I want to get to know you. Friends is a good place to start. After we're friends, we can reevaluate things."

"Boy, kiss my butt," she said, pulling her door open and tossing her bag into the passenger seat.

Gator grinned. "We'll get to that, but can I get your number first?"

She was considering it. He could tell because she closed her eyes and said nothing for a few seconds. "Twenty-four, eighteen," Tiffany said, getting into the door and closing the door.

Gator humped his shoulders. Tiffany started the car and backed out of the driveway while he stared at her trying to understand what she meant. *Alright, if that's all you are going to give me. I'll take it.* He waved as she drove away.

~Cougar~

"What's the house number?" Cougar asked Diego as they turned on the street where Bunker's house was located.

"Fifty-six-twenty," he replied. "It should be on your side. Those are even numbers."

Cougar slowed down so they could see the house numbers even though her GPS guided them. "You have arrived. Your destination is on the left," the device told her.

She turned into the driveway, parking behind the garage. They got out and walked to the door, knocking and ringing the bell. They waited and then did it again. "I don't think she's going to answer."

Diego walked back towards the garage. "She knew we were coming, right?"

"That's what Fox said when Kelly asked if I could come get her." The door was all wood, and there was no window near it. Cougar couldn't see into the house.

Diego was jumping to peek into the windows near the top of the garage door. "There's no car in the garage," he called to Cougar.

"Fox gave me her phone number. Let's see if she'll answer the phone." She took out her phone and dialed the number.

Diego had returned to the porch. "Do you hear that?" Cougar took the phone from her ear. They could faintly hear a phone ringing inside the house.

When the call went to voicemail, Cougar hit the end button. "We might need to break in."

"I'll see if I can get in around back," Diego said, moving off the porch and around one side of the house.

Cougar continued to knock and ring the bell but got no answer. Diego returned a few minutes later. "Did you find a way in?"

"I could get over the fence and break a window, but the alarm might go off," he said, pointing to the ADT sign partially hidden in the flower bed near the door.

"I don't think we should do that in this neighborhood. We look suspicious enough, peeping through windows and walking around the border of the house." Sure enough, a woman strolled by walking her dog. "Excuse me," Cougar called out from across the law. "Do you know the Bunkers? I had an appointment with Mrs. Bunker, but she's not answering the door or her phone. I was wondering if you've seen her today?" The lady looked at both Cougar and Diego as if assessing them. Cougar walked across the grass to the woman with Diego following her.

"Do you have some kind of identification?"

Cougar pulled out a business card and handed it to her. "I'm an advocate for children."

The woman looked at the card and then into Cougar's eyes. "Are they adopting another kid?" She smiled when she asked. "This would be their third one. Claudia and Harrison are such good people."

Cougar could see the admiration on the woman's face. She didn't want to give away that she had no idea that the Bunkers had adopted children. "They are indeed."

"Those boys are lucky to have been placed with Claudia and Harrison. It would be nice if they got a girl this time around."

"Have you seen her today?"

"Yes, about an hour ago. She took the kids and left the house. I was in the front yard pulling up weeds when she drove past."

"Thank you. I guess she must have forgotten about the appointment."

"Oh, no problem at all," she said, walking down the sidewalk.

They returned to the car. She dialed Kelly's number instead of going through Fox to talk to her. Cougar didn't see the point of having him as a go-between. She gave the woman who answered the phone her name and waited while her assistant transferred her.

"Do you have Mrs. Bunker?"

"She's not here, and it doesn't look like foul play. I spoke to a neighbor who said she saw her driving away about an hour ago."

"Where could she have gone?" Kelly asked, not expecting an answer. "I'll have someone track her phone."

"Don't bother. I called it when we got here. Her phone is in the house. We could hear it ringing."

"Why would she leave like that?"

"That's a good question. We could get into the house, but they have an alarm. If we break in, we'll have to explain it to the police when they show up."

"No. I don't want the police involved. What about the people who got into Bunker's office? Do you think they could get into the house?"

"I'm sure they could, but we'd have to wait for them to get here. This is not the neighborhood for an African American woman and Hispanic man to sit with nothing to do until our help arrives."

"Hold on. I'll call Mr. Bunker and see if there is a hidden spare key."

"Don't forget to ask him for the alarm code and location of the panel if there is a key we can use."

"Okay. I'll call you back in a few minutes."

"So, we're just gonna sit here in the car until she calls back?"

"Yup," Cougar said, looking in her rearview mirror. They were being watched from across the street. "If she doesn't call back in five minutes, we'll go to the Starbucks we passed a few blocks ago."

Kelly hadn't given her all the details, but it sounded like she believed someone in the police department might be involved in this somehow.

Chapter Twenty-Three

~Kelly~

The minute she got off the phone with Bailey, Kelly dialed her father's number. "Hello?"

"I need to speak to Mr. Bunker," she said, not bothering with pleasantries.

"Is my wife safe?"

"I don't know. My people are at your house right now, but your wife isn't. They tried calling her, and it seemed she had left her phone in the house. Where is she?"

"I don't know. She should have been there. I told her you were sending someone to pick her and the kids up. Let me call her."

"Mr. Bunker. Is there a key hidden at your house that they can access to get in?"

"No."

"They can get in by other means, but they'll need the alarm code."

"I can turn it off with the app on my phone. There's a window to the bathroom behind the garage. It should be cracked open. Maybe they can get in through there."

"Okay. I'll let them know. Turn off the alarm as soon as we get off the phone. Now, let me speak to my father."

"Yeah," her father said once he had the phone.

"Send me your address. I'll come over as soon as I can. I think Mr. Bunker and I better talk sooner rather than later."

"Okay," her father said before she ended the call. She grabbed her purse and left her office while calling Bailey to tell her about the alarm and window.

~Cougar~

After speaking with Kelly about the open window, Cougar and Diego carefully moved around the house, ensuring no one saw them. "It's open, just like she said," Cougar commented as they looked at the window. It was a little high off the ground, but they could still get in through it.

Diego pulled a switchblade from his pocket, sliding it between the screen border and the window frame. With a flick of his wrist, the screen popped out. Cougar took it and leaned it against the house. "I'll give you a boost," he told her, cupping his hands together for her to put her foot in.

She put her foot in place with her hands on his shoulders. Cougar pushed off the ground with her other foot as Diego lifted her. She grabbed the edge of the windowsill while he supported her. Then with Diego's help, she could stick her head and shoulders through the window and rest her behind on the sill. Then she carefully climbed through, stepping into the space in front of the toilet. She poked her head back out the window. "Put the screen back in place and meet me at the front door."

As soon as the screen was back in place, Cougar let the window down, putting the lock in place. While moving through the house, Cougar noted that all the doors were open except one. She pushed it open. It was a home office.

When she opened the door for Diego, he said, "I think we're good. I didn't see anyone watching us."

"Let's make it quick. I don't want to get surprised by the cops because someone saw us."

They moved through the house quickly. There was nothing out of place that they could tell. Cougar went into one of the kid's rooms. Diego went into the master bedroom. Some toys were strewn around the kids' rooms, but it looked like a normal kid mess. Cougar opened closets and drawers and looked in the closets.

She also checked the hall bathroom and noticed no toothbrushes or toothpaste. She returned to the hall as Diego came out of the master bedroom.

"I don't think she was kidnapped. There are empty hangers, and a few drawers were pulled out and looked empty," he told Cougar.

"Yeah, it's the same in the children's rooms. Plus, there are no toothbrushes in the holder on the wall by the sink, and I didn't see any toothpaste. I think she took off on her own." They walked through the rest of the house together.

In the kitchen, they found her cell phone on the counter. Diego picked it up. "The screen is locked with biometrics."

"If she left of her own free will, she left it behind because she didn't want to be tracked while using it."

"The question is, did she do that to keep the bad guys or the cops from finding her," Diego said, putting the phone down.

"Good question." Cougar picked up the phone, sliding it into her pocket. "Maybe Rabbit can get something off of it. Let's go. You drive, and I'll call her and tell her to meet us at the clubhouse."

"What about Kelly?"

"I'll call her after I talk to Rabbit."

Chapter Twenty-Four

~Harrison~

Harrison was pacing the small living room floor where Mr. Garza had taken him. Claudia and his children were missing. In his mind, there was no mistaking that Haji was behind it. Somehow he had figured out he was planning to go to the police. He had taken his wife and kids to keep him quiet.

Mr. Garza came in from the backyard, where he had been on the phone for a while. "You're gonna wear a hole in the carpet."

He stopped walking. "I'm just worried about my wife and children." Harrison's message tone played. He pulled the phone from his pocket. He had a new message from a number he didn't know.

I'm sorry, but I can't take the chance of losing Kyle. You and I both know that's exactly what will happen. Forgive me for running off, Claudia.

Harrison slumped into a nearby chair, staring at the phone. He was relieved that his wife hadn't been kidnapped, but he was distraught that she had chosen to take their children and run from their problems.

Someone knocked on the front door. "Go in the bedroom and stay there until I tell you to come out," Mr. Garza told him as he pulled a gun from his waistband and moved towards the house's entryway.

Harrison moved quickly into the bedroom and closed the door, putting his ear to it so he could listen. He heard talking. It was a woman. "Mr. Bunker, you can come out," Mr. Garza yelled.

Harrison opened the door to find the woman he'd seen on the news after the women were freed from the factory.

"Ms. Lewis?"

She smiled, extending her hand to him. "Mr. Bunker, I wish we were meeting under better circumstances."

"Me too," Harrison said, shaking her hand. He considered whether to tell her about the text from his wife. He didn't like the idea of her being alone when someone might be trying to silence him. They would use his family to get to him if they caught her.

When she released his hand, Ms. Lewis blew air out of her mouth. "The people I sent to get your wife got in through the window you told me about. They found your wife's phone in the kitchen. There was no note from her, but it looked like she had left on her own. It looked like she packed some things in a hurry. It made sense because she knew that people were on the way to get her. Her phone was locked with a biometric passkey. They would like to attempt to crack it and see if there are any clues as to where she is going. Do you have any idea where she might be headed?"

Harrison shook his head. "No, but she sent me this message a few minutes before you knocked on the door." He handed her his phone.

After reading the text, Harrison watched as Ms. Lewis took a screenshot of the message and number. Then she dialed a number on her phone. "Bailey, Mrs. Bunker sent her husband a message a few minutes ago. I'm forwarding it to you. I'm pretty sure she used a burner phone since you have hers. I don't know if it will help us locate her."

Ms. Lewis was quiet as the person on the phone spoke. Then she said, "Okay. I understand. Let me know the minute you find out anything." She handed him his phone. "My people aren't sure if they will be able to track her down if she's using a throw-away phone, but they are going to try." She turned to her father. "Can I have a minute alone with him?"

"Sure," her dad said, going through the patio door to the backyard and closing it behind himself.

"Mr. Bunker, sit down."

Harrison sat in the armchair next to the couch, where she took a seat. "Do you have any idea why your wife would take off like this?"

"Before I get into this, I need some assurances from you."

"Like what?"

"I need your word that you will not charge my wife with any crime related to what I've done. She is innocent."

"Mr. Bunker, right now, I have no reason to prosecute your wife, but I'm not sure I can make that promise until you have told me everything I need to know."

"I'm not telling you anything until I have your word that Claudia will be allowed to raise our son."

Chapter Twenty- Five

~Kelly~

Son? Based on their conversations before, Harrison had used the word children. Now, he was using the words' 'his son'. It wasn't just a slip of the tongue. Kelly didn't want to tell him she had the files he'd kept in his office. "I promise I will do all I can to keep your wife from going to prison, but I need you to tell me everything."

He stared at her for a while before speaking. "Alright," he said, his shoulders sagging as if he was done carrying the weight of his crimes. He told her about his son and Haji before telling her about all the children he'd placed with families.

"What was your involvement with the women, the mothers of these babies?"

"I was not involved with any of them. I have no idea what happened to them. I did what Haji demanded of me. I found homes for the kids, homes where the parents wouldn't want to know where these kids came from because they were desperate to be parents. I have the records of each child I found a family for."

"That's not entirely true, is it? There was no record for Michelle Leeland's son." She watched as the realization dawned on his face. "I have copies of the records from your safe and computer. Mr. Bunker, have you and your wife raised her son as your own?"

She watched his Adam's apple move as he swallowed, and he looked away from her. "Yes, but I never told Claudia where the child came from. Well, not until a few days ago. She implored me to contact you and tell you what I know, and I was going to do that, but your father showed up at my office before I could reach out to you. You have to understand," he said, moving forward to sit on the edge of the chair. "We were older when we met and wanted a family. We adopted a child when we first got together, but he died later. We were waiting to adopt when I was told to find a home for Kyle. He was one of the first kids I was told to place. I had no choice but to take him home. It would be for a few days, but I saw how having him affected Claudia. She was happier than she had ever been. I knew that they were going to use Michelle as a midwife. I figured at some point she would either be sent away with the other women or they would – kill her. Either way, I figured she would want her son to be in a loving home, and my wife loved him immensely."

"That's why she ran away. She couldn't stand the thought of giving him up," Kelly said. "I understand, but Michelle Leeland is free, and her son has to be returned to her. When your wife contacts you again, it would be in your best interest and hers to convince your wife to bring the boy back. One of the men in charge of these women died in his jail cell, and your family could be in danger. We can't protect her if she's out there alone."

"I know. I will do what I can to convince her to do the right thing."

"Are you sure that you don't have any idea of where she would go? What about friends and family?"

"Her life has always been about the kids. Her parents are dead. She was an only child but has an aunt in Phoenix, Arizona. She's in a nursing home, so I can't imagine her going there, but I suppose you should check with Barbara."

Kelly got Aunt Barbara's last name and the name of the home she was in. She stood up. She went outside the patio door to speak to her father. "I have to go. I'm taking Mr. Bunker with me. Thank you for your help."

"You're taking a big chance of the world finding out about me. You know that, don't you?"

He was right. Her career would be ruined if anyone found out that her father was a convicted felon running a drug empire. She nodded. "I doubt that anyone will put it together. At worst, they'll find out I know you, but not that we're related. It's not like your name is on my birth certificate."

"No, it's not. I did that to protect you all."

Kelly sighed. "Anyway, I appreciate you coming to the rescue for me," she turned and returned to the house. "Let's go, Mr. Bunker."

Chapter Twenty-Six

~Panther~

When he left Mike's Gym, Panther returned to his office to attend a meeting with one of the few clients that weren't associated with the club. When that meeting was over, he walked his client out. To his surprise, someone was sitting in one of the two chairs he kept in the outer office. "Thank you, Mr. Carter," his departing client said as Panther held the door open for him.

He rarely got new clients, but most called before coming to his office. He turned to the woman, who stood and spoke. "Do you remember me?"

She looked familiar, but Panther couldn't place her right off. He shook his head. "No, I'm sorry."

"You carried me out of the factory."

Panther's mouth dropped open. It had only been a few weeks, but Michelle looked different, healthier, and cleaner. "Michelle?"

The corners of her mouth lifted slightly. "Yes. I'm sorry for stalking you, but I need your help."

"Stalking me?" Panther's eyebrows rose.

"Yes. I went to the gym, planning to talk to the guy I saw on the news, but when I saw you, I realized that I'd rather talk to you, so I followed you when you left the gym."

Panther opened the door to his office. "Come in and sit down." Once they were both seated in the chairs before his desk, he asked, "What do you need my help with?"

"Finding my son," she told him.

Panther knew there was no record of Michelle's child among Bunker's files. He wouldn't tell her that. Even though she looked better, he could see she was at her wit's end, and he couldn't blame her. "The FBI has taken over the case. They are working to reunite the children with their families. I can put you in touch with them."

Michelle was vehemently shaking her head. "No. I don't trust anyone but you. You have to help me," she said, grabbing his hands. "I've talked to the police and don't feel like they care. My own family doesn't think I will ever get my baby back. My sister-in-law even said that I should come to grips with reality. I will never stop looking for him, but I need help."

Looking into her eyes and feeling the grip of her hands, he could see her desperation. He couldn't tell her no. "Do you have any information that might help locate him?"

Michelle released his hands, covering the smile on her face. A few tears fell from her eyes. Panther got up and went to the rack where his jacket was hanging. He took the pocket square and handed it to her. She wiped her eyes and then told him everything she could remember about the day her son was born and the days after.

It wasn't much to go on, but Panther wouldn't tell her that. "Ms. Leeland, I will do what I can but can't promise anything."

"I understand. I'm grateful that you are willing to help. I don't have much, but I will pay you for your services."

"That's not necessary," he told her, standing up.

"There has to be something I can do to pay you."

"We can discuss that at another time. Let me see what I can find out for now, okay?" He took her number and address down before walking her to the door of the outer office.

"Thank you," she said before leaving.

Chapter Twenty-Seven

~Hippo~

After his mother left, Hippo spent the afternoon thinking about what she told him about keeping secrets. She was right. Starting a relationship with Sameera while keeping the secret that he was recently in love with Cougar wasn't a good idea. *I'll tell her tonight after dinner. Hopefully, she will understand.*

In the past few months, he had watched Carl and Eden have issues that could have been avoided if they had trusted each other instead of thinking they were protecting each other. Cougar and Diego had the same kind of drama. Diego hid who he was from her, and their relationship almost ended before it started.

Hippo didn't expect to have a perfect and flawless relationship with Sameera. Still, he didn't want to be the cause of any misunderstandings that could ruin what he believed they could have together.

She was beautiful, smart, and fearless. She deserved the truth.

He was in the kitchen when Sameera and her sister returned home. "Hello, ladies," he said as they entered the kitchen. Both were carrying grocery bags.

They sat them on the counter. "Hey, handsome," Sameera said as she unpacked the bags. "I got bacon and some other stuff I thought we could use." She glanced at the stove. "Did you cook dinner?"

"Momma came by and spent the afternoon with me. She started dinner before she left."

"Aw, I hate that I missed her." She turned to her sister. Ms. Dottie is great. You have to meet her while you're here."

Haimari smiled, "That would be nice. So far, everyone Sammi introduced me to is wonderful."

"Who all did you meet besides Mike and Warthog?" Hippo asked as Haimari handed the food from the bags to Sameera to put away.

"Panther."

Hippo noticed the rise of her cheeks and the flush of color that spread through her face.

"Yeah," Sameera said, closing the pantry door. "He's taking her to dinner on Wednesday to give us some quality time for Valentine's Day."

"That's nice of him."

"Maybe, but I think he has his own motives for doing so," Sameera said, grinning at Haimari.

"Oh, shut up," Haimari said, grinning widely.

"I'm going to take a quick shower, and then we can sit down and eat if everything is ready?"

"It is," Hippo told her. "It's just steak, baked potatoes, and a salad."

"I'll help you take the food to the table," Haimari told Hippo as Sameera left the room.

As they prepared the table for dinner, Hippo asked, "What do you think about Sameera's training and becoming a member of my bike club?"

"Honestly, I learned a lot about my sister today. Sammi has always done things her way, but I never understood how determined she was until I watched her learn how to kick butt today. Seeing her with a gun in her hand was a bit shocking, but she's good, and if she's going to be involved in dangerous things, she should know how to defend and protect herself. In my head, I've always pictured her just having fun and partying. I had no idea that she had ever been in any danger. I'm happy that she's found herself and feels good about what she's doing, but our parents will never accept this."

"Maybe they will," Hippo hoped.

"No. They are traditionalists. I'm certain they'll disown her if they find out about it." She sighed and sat down in one of the chairs around the table. "They will forbid me from seeing her. They may have disowned me for coming here."

"Look, God knows I've had problems with my mother, but your parents love you both. They'll just need time to accept things, that's all."

"I'd like to believe that, but I know them, and they will not accept a relationship with you."

"Why, because I'm black, or because I'm a biker, American?"

"For all those reasons, you are not who they picked for her. I'm sorry to say it, but it's the truth. They will not accept her relationship with you. Don't get me wrong, they love her. I've been trying to mend this rift between them, and they would allow her to come home, but there would be conditions, and I don't think Sammi would agree to them."

"What do you mean?"

"They arranged a suitable match for her, and she took off, not once, but twice. If they accept her back into their lives, she will have to remain hidden because of the embarrassment she caused them. Now, I've done the same thing. It took Sammi telling me what I already knew to open my eyes. Raja is not what I want for my future. I realized that I did not love Raja and that marrying him would be a mistake. That's why I came here. Sammi has made a life for herself, and I need to do the same because I'm not going back."

The emotions rolling off of Haimari were palpable. "Haimari, you have nothing to worry about. You will find your way through life and are

147

welcome to stay here as long as you like." The smile she gave him was small but filled with relief. "Now, let's get the rest of the food in here. Sammi will be down any minute."

Chapter Twenty-Eight

~Claudia~

As she turned onto the road to her father's old ranch house, Claudia glanced in the rearview mirror to check on the boys. They were both sleeping. She knew what she was doing was wrong. She shouldn't have taken off like that, but she had panicked at the thought of having to give Kyle up.

Claudia stopped the car in front of the house. It still looked in good shape. She and Harrison hadn't been to the house in a long time. It was where they planned to live once the boys were older. She knew that she could only stay there for a day or two. Harrison would eventually figure out that this was where she had taken the kids. Maybe he wouldn't tell the D.A. about it. He loved Kyle as much as she did.

She got out of the car, leaving the boys inside while she went around back and started the generator. Then she carried in each child, and on her final trip, she brought in some of their things and the fast food she stopped to get them to eat for dinner.

Claudia stood at the bedroom door, looking at her sons as they lay curled up on the bed in the main bedroom.

"What am I doing?" she whispered. She was sure Harrison was beside himself with worry. She closed the door and went into the kitchen, sitting at the round table. She took out the phone she had purchased at target and dialed his number.

"Claudia?" Harrison answered after two rings. "Are you okay? Where are you?"

"Honey, we're fine. I'm not going to talk long. I just needed to tell you that I'm sorry."

"Claudia, please tell me where you are."

"I can't do that. If I do, I will lose him forever, and you know it. I took the money from our joint account. We'll need it. I just wanted you to know that I love you," she said, ending the call.

~The Beasts~

The phone sitting next to Rabbit's computer set up rang. She glanced into the office where Harrison Bunker sat with Kelly. When they arrived, she cloned Harrison's phone. Cougar and Mike sat on her left and right sides.

While they listened to his brief call with Claudia, Rabbit tried to triangulate her position from the towers that her phone pinged. When Claudia hung up, Cougar and Mike looked at Rabbit expectantly. "The call wasn't long enough," she told them. The most I can tell you is that she's still in Texas. We have to keep her on the phone longer."

"What if she doesn't call back?" Cougar asked.

"I think she will," Mike said. "I could hear the regret in her voice. Regret for disappearing and not wanting to give Kyle back to his mother. She'll call back. I'm sure of it."

"If she does, and if you can keep her on the phone long enough, I can, at the very least, give you maybe a fifty-mile radius of her location."

"If she's using a burner phone, how can you track it. I thought that was the whole point of getting one, that they couldn't be traced," Kelly said as she joined them.

"That's a huge misconception," Rabbit told her. "Burner phones are only untraceable if you use them once and toss them. Most people don't know that. It also depends on how you purchased the phone. It would be harder to track if she paid cash for it. Which is what she did."

"How do you know that?"

Rabbit sat back in her chair. "I hacked into their personal accounts. She wasn't using credit cards and took a large amount of cash from the bank. She's not planning to turn the boy over. She's on the run. If she tosses that phone before we figure out where she is, we might never find her."

"Fuck," Kelly said, shaking her head.

"And he doesn't have any idea where she would go?" Mike asked Kelly.

"If he does, he's not telling me anything," she answered.

"Then we need to think of another way to get the information out of him," Cougar said, glancing at Harrison, who slouched in the office a few feet away, staring into space.

Chapter Twenty-Nine

~Hippo~

They were in the kitchen after dinner when Hippo said, "Sammi, I need to talk to you. I thought we could sit on the back patio. It's cool out, but we could light the firepit."

"That sounds nice," Sameera told him as she loaded the dishwasher.

"Do you mind if I read one of the books by the bed?" Haimari asked.

"Help yourself," Sameera said as she closed the door to the dishwasher. "Let me grab a blanket to throw over your legs," she told Hippo.

"Okay, I'll meet you in the backyard," he said, moving towards the door to the yard.

Once he was outside, he was glad that she offered to get a blanket, the air was cool, and as the sun lowered in the sky, it got cooler. The fire pit was full of wood from the last time he'd cleaned it after sitting out back on a cool night.

Sameera joined him, covering his legs before taking the lighter and lighting the wood in the pit. Then she sat down in one of the wicker chairs. Hippo moved around to the right side of the chair. He used his left hand to hold hers.

"I talked with my mom today about honesty and the importance of starting a relationship on the right foot. There is something that I have actively been keeping from you since we met, and I want to tell you the truth because I've seen how secrets can destroy relationships. I want us to be completely honest with each other from here on out." He looked into her eyes. "The reason that I'm single now is that the woman that I thought I was in love with ended our relationship. I was involved with Cougar for a long time, but she ended it last year."

Sameera didn't say anything at first. She let his hand go, rubbing her face as his words sank in.

"Cougar?" She asked, standing up. She took a few steps from him. "I don't believe this. Why didn't she tell me that?"

"I asked her not to. I asked everyone not to mention it. I wanted us to get to know each other a little better before we started discussing our past relationships."

"Yeah, but I've never had one. Why didn't you tell me this the other day when I told you about being a virgin? Do you understand how embarrassing this is for me? I've talked candidly with her about my feelings and fears about getting involved with you." Sameera was shaking her head. "I'm so hurt right now."

"I'm sorry," Hippo said, closing his eyes.

"So am I," she said, returning to the house.

Sorry for allowing me into your life? I hope not. He wanted to stop her, but he saw she needed time. He would give her that; hopefully, they could get past it.

~Sameera~

Sameera went upstairs after leaving Hippo in the yard. Haimari came out of the bathroom and sat on the bed.

"Couple time over already?" Sameera closed her eyes and flopped back on the bed. "What's wrong?" She asked, coming over to sit near her sister.

"He told me that his ex-girlfriend was the woman I was staying with when I returned to town. I had no idea. I'm so embarrassed. I have talked to this woman honestly about my hopes and fears where he's concerned. He's kept this from me until now."

"Really?" Haimari said. "You can't be upset with him for that. You've been keeping your wealth from him. You told me so yourself. That's no different from what he did. In the big picture, Sammi, does it matter? Their relationship is over, right?" She didn't wait for Sameera to answer. She continued. "I think it says a lot about him that he told you now. You need to go down there and come clean yourself."

Sameera sat up, looking at Haimari. Her sister was right. She had been keeping secrets too. Hippo was also right. If they were going to have a future, they needed to come clean and be understanding. "You're right," she said, standing up.

"And just so you know, you don't have to sleep up here with me. I appreciate you wanting to be there for me, but I'll be alright if you want to sleep with him."

Sameera stared at her sister with her mouth hanging open. "Haimari, this is where I've been sleeping since I moved into the house. Hippo and I have never been together."

"What?"

"I'm still untouched."

Haimari started to laugh until she realized that her sister was serious. "Are you kidding me? I just assumed that while you've been on your own, you had – you know, done it with someone."

Sameera shook her head. "No."

"Well, crap. I was hoping you could tell me if what they say about black men is true." When her sister continued staring at her as if she didn't know what she meant, Haimari said, "You know – that they are well endowed and are great in bed?"

Sameera shook her head. "Is that why you want to go out with Panther?"

Haimari raised one eyebrow and smiled. "Maybe."

"We have a lot to discuss, but we'll get into that later. I need to go talk to Kenny."

Hippo was still sitting outside. She came out and took the same seat. "I'm sorry for walking away from you. I am embarrassed by all of this, but I've been keeping a secret from you too. I like you a lot, but I was afraid to tell you this because people start to act differently around me when they find out about it. They always have." She paused and took his hand as he did. She looked him in the eye. "My parents are rich."

Hippo smiled. "Is that your secret, that your family is rich?"

"My parents are rich, like Elon Musk and the Walton family. They're not famous or in the public eye the way those people are. I don't consider myself rich even though I have a trust fund that would more than provide for me and generations of my family."

"Did you keep this from me because you thought I would be more interested in your money than you?"

She shook her head. "I don't know, but the moment people find out about my family's wealth, they start to behave differently, and I didn't want that to happen. I don't consider myself rich. I haven't used any of the money in my trust. I wanted to make my own way in the world. Honestly, I figured that my parents had disowned me. I didn't know until I saw Haimari in Florida that I could still access the funds. I won't, but I thought that they would have cut me off financially after I ran away from the arranged marriage they set up for me." She sighed, waiting for him to say something.

He squeezed her hand. "I feel silly thinking I was saving you by letting you stay here." He chuckled, "According to what you've just told me, I'm a pauper." He smiled. "I don't care about the money. I'm glad you told me, and I hope you can forgive me for not being upfront with you about my past relationship with Cougar. I still want to move forward with you."

"You do?" Sameera said softly.

"Yes," Hippo said, tugging her closer. "I'm falling for you, Sameera."

She smiled so big that her face hurt. "Really?"

Hippo leaned closer, brushing his lips against hers. Sameera closed her eyes and gave herself over to the joy and excitement that flowed from his mouth, filling her with the possibilities that awaited them.

Chapter Thirty

~Panther~

He was brushing his teeth when Panther got the text from Cougar asking that The Beasts come to a meeting at the clubhouse if they were available. He intended to go to his office and work, but he could take the time to attend the meeting to see what was going on.

He finished dressing and left his condo, heading to the clubhouse. He reminded himself that he needed to speak with Cougar and Mike about Michelle's visit to his office the day before.

As he got out of his car and went to the entrance to the clubhouse, a few women going into the gym smiled and waved to him.

He reciprocated, "Good morning, ladies."

"Looking good," one of them called back to him.

He grinned and went inside. He was used to women flirting with him. He was good-looking no matter what he put on, but for some reason women seemed to pay more attention to him in his business attire than in his jeans or leather pants.

Several Beasts were sitting around the table, including Sameera.

"Morning, everyone," he said, taking a seat. Mike and Cougar stood with Carl and Bear, talking a few feet from the table.

A few more of his club brothers came in and took a seat.

"What's going on?" Cheetah asked when he sat beside Panther.

"Not sure. I just got here a few minutes before you."

"Alright, everybody," Cougar said as she and the guys she had been talking to all turned to face the table of members waiting to find out what the meeting was about. "Our problem is that yesterday one of the men arrested from the factory was found hanging in his cell. Ms. Lewis doesn't think that it was a suicide. She also thinks that Mr. Bunker is in danger. She arranged for someone to pick him up, so we have him in our custody to protect him until we can ascertain the real danger." Cougar went on to explain that Mrs. Bunker had taken off. "We now know that she left because she doesn't want to give up the child she raised. Kyle Bunker is Michelle Leeland's son."

Mike took over from there. "We are trying to track her. Along with Rabbit, Amethyst has been informed, and the FBI are doing everything they can to locate her by watching for her car and any activity on her credit cards and Bank accounts. The biggest problem is that she has taken a large amount of cash from their accounts. She has the means to get lost, and we don't want that to happen."

"Are we tracking her cell phone?" A member asked.

"She left her phone behind, but she has contacted her husband. We think she is using a burner phone. Rabbit has cloned Mr. Bunker's cell, and she will try to triangulate her position if she contacts her husband again. I need you all to be ready to go after her when we get an idea of where she is. Right now, we can only tell she hasn't left the state.

We figured out that much during her last contact with her husband."

"Are you planning to tell Michelle? I ask because Michelle came to my office yesterday for help finding her child. She said she came to me because she trusts us or me specifically to get it done," Panther told them.

"Until we can locate him and then have the DNA test done, I don't think we should tell her about this," Cougar said.

"I agree," Mike added. "Since she's come to you specifically, why don't you stay in contact with her? We'll keep this development under our hats for now."

"No problem." Panther listened to the rest of their update on the issue. He could keep this to himself, but he felt that Michelle might lose it because of the time it might take to get her child back. He just hoped that it all worked out.

Chapter Thirty-One

~Michelle~

She was making coffee when her sister-in-law, Karen, came into the kitchen.

"Good morning," Michelle greeted her.

"What are your plans for the day?"

Michelle sipped from her cup before she answered. "I'm not sure. Yesterday, I spoke to one of those men that found me. I asked for his help to find my son." Karen sighed dramatically as she closed the door to the fridge. Michelle shook her head slightly. "What?" She asked though she didn't need to. She knew what Karen thought.

"I just think you should work toward getting your life together."

Michelle sat her mug on the counter. "I am."

"No. You're dwelling on something that you should move on from."

Michelle turned. "Move on? I can't move on until I have my son. Don't you understand that?"

"You may never get him back, and you need to face that."

"Why would you say something like that?"

"Because it's the truth. God is the only one who knows where he is or if he's even still alive. You need to get a job and – and – get your own place. You need to do something productive instead of sitting around the house feeling sorry for yourself."

Michelle wanted to strangle Karen. How could anyone be so uncaring? She picked up her mug and left the room. When Ryan wasn't around, her sister-in-law made it clear that she wanted Michelle out of their house.

They barely knew each other. Ryan had just started dating her when Michelle was snatched off the street. She had no idea what her brother saw in the woman.

Karen seemed bitter and controlling, and before meeting her, Ryan was independent and had a strong mind. Now, it appeared he was a man who allowed his wife to rule the roost. Karen was right about one thing. Michelle needed to get a job and her own place. She didn't want to have anything to do with raising her child around this woman.

~Cassidy~

There was only one person at the shop when Cassidy got there. "Where are Goose and Moose?" She asked as Gazelle let her in.

"They went to a club meeting. They'll be here soon."

"Why didn't you go? Aren't you in the club too?"

Cassidy knew this, but Gazelle hadn't been very social since she started working there. She hoped she could get her to open up.

"You don't have a key, and there was no way to know how long the meeting would last. So, I came to work. The guys will update me on what was discussed."

"Can I ask you a question?"

"You just did," she answered, moving back towards the workroom.

"I guess I did, but I wanted to know how you got your – uh- name in the club?"

She paused, holding the door open. "Gazelle's have to be fast to outrun predators, and I like crotch rockets over the style of a Harley, and when they welcomed me into the club, that's the name they gave me."

Cassidy didn't get a chance to say anything further. Gazelle went into the workroom, closing the door behind herself. ***Well, she answered my question. That's the most she's said to me since I got here.***

She expected things to be easier than this. Cassidy thought that she would charm their pants off and they would spill all of their secrets, but getting anything worth taking to the chief was hard. She moved around the counter and began getting ready to open the business.

Chapter Thirty-Two

~Panther~

After leaving the clubhouse, Panther stopped and grabbed a coffee and a slice of iced lemon pound cake before going to his office. He was trying to unlock his office door while juggling his things when someone cleared their throat. "Can I help you with that?" Michelle asked from behind him.

He stepped aside, releasing the keys into her hand. While she unlocked and opened the door for him, Panther took a long look at her. She looked great. Her hair was pulled back from her face. She was wearing make-up, and her dress was stylish. "Thank you," he said, following her inside.

She opened the inner door for him and stood there while he sat his things on the desk. "I bet you're wondering why I'm here."

"Do you want to tell me why?"

Michelle laced her fingers together and fidgeted. "I noticed you don't have anyone at the desk out there. I – I need a job. I can't go back to working in the morgue. I just can't. I was wondering if you needed some help. I can type and answer phones."

Panther listened as Michelle ran off a list of things she could help him with. When she stopped, he sat down in his chair.

"Michelle, I'm not a full-time accountant. I'm not sure that this would be a good place for you to be." He saw the devastation in her eyes. "Maybe you can help me through tax season, but after that, I can't guarantee that I can keep you employed."

Her cheeks rose. "I can live with that. I have to start somewhere, right?"

Panther nodded, smiling at her. They discussed what he would pay her and what days and hours Michelle could come in to help him. Then he got up and showed her all that he needed help with for the day. She was smiling and happy, and he was glad he could help her. More than anything, he wanted to be able to bring her son home to her.

~Hippo~

"Morning," Hippo said to Haimari when she entered the kitchen.

"Good morning."

"Sameera said not to wake you. The club called a meeting, and she said she didn't want you just sitting around the gym waiting for her. Are you hungry?"

She shook her head. "No, but a cup of coffee would be great."

"The pods are next to the Keurig, and mugs are in the cabinet above it."

"Are things okay between you two? I was asleep when she came to bed," Haimari told him as she began to make her coffee.

"Yes. There are no more secrets between us," he said, smiling. "And I got a kiss." He should feel silly saying it, but he didn't. He felt like a superhero who had gotten the girl of his dreams. He also realized that Haimari was there because she had trouble with her fiancé. "I'm sorry if I'm being insensitive. I know why you came to visit. Are you okay?"

While her cup filled, she turned so that she was facing him. "Actually, I am. My parents haven't bothered to call, and they haven't responded to my text messages. The crazy part is that I always assumed that they had tried to speak to Sameera after she left. I thought that she was the one who refused to speak to them, but I'm beginning to think I was wrong." She got her coffee and added sugar.

"They are probably upset, but I'm sure they care," Hippo told her, thinking about the problems he had with his mother. "What about your fiancé? Have you heard from him?"

She snorted. "Ex-fiancé. Yes, he's been blowing my phone up. So much so that I turned the sound off. The texts and voice messages were – mean."

"Mean?"

"Yeah, Raja is a bit domineering and sexist, if you know what I mean?"

Hippo didn't like the sound of that. "He didn't threaten you, did he?"

"No."

Hippo didn't believe her. "Well, you are more than safe here, understand?" She nodded her head. "Since you will be hanging out at the house with me today, I could use your help with my Valentine's gift for your sister."

"Of course," Haimari said, smiling as she lifted her mug to her lips. "What do you need me to do?" Hippo explained, and when Haimari started to smile, he knew it was a good plan. "She'll love it."

Chapter Thirty-Three

~Sameera~

Although her training with Mike had been delayed, it was not canceled. They worked on her defense techniques, and Mike had her work with Rhino lifting weights. Then she would be excused to go to Warthog's range for her gun training.

It was the first time she had spent any real time with the big guy. She felt a little intimidated by him. He was huge, like a Rhino, and covered in tattoos. What was amusing once they started was that the big beast of a man was soft-spoken and very encouraging. "You're doing great," he said as she followed his instructions with the dumbbells. "Mike is really impressed with your progress. You learn quickly, and you're stronger than you look."

"Do you – guys always- discuss how - I'm doing?" She asked, blowing out the air between her reps.

"Not typically, but Mike and I have been discussing your abilities, and we think that you should take some yoga classes, and then we'll get someone to teach you martial arts."

"Really – why?"

"It's something that he thinks you'll be good at. Then he wants to pay you to train the rest of the club."

"Seriously?"

"Yeah."

Sameera set the hand weights down, smiling. It was something that she had never considered. *A martial arts expert? I like it.*

"What do you think of the idea?" Rhino asked, motioning for her to move to the bench. "Lay down," he said, standing behind the weights to spot her.

"I'm excited to do it."

"Good," Rhino said. Then he instructed her on her form and explained how this weight training would strengthen her shoulders, chest, and arms.

She worked out with him until Rhino told her they were done for the day. She was gathering her things to leave when her phone rang. She dug through her bag, trying to find it before it stopped ringing.

"Hello?" she answered without looking at the caller ID. Sameera figured that it was either her sister or Hippo calling. She was shocked by who the actual caller was.

"Let me speak to my fiancé," Raja demanded. "I know she's with you."

"Actually, she's not," Sameera said.

"Don't play with me, Sameera. Let me speak to her right now!"

Sameera calmly replied, "Have you tried calling her?"

"She won't answer," he growled.

"Then maybe you should take the hint, Raja. Haimari doesn't want to talk to you, and since she came here, I don't think she wants to marry you either."

"Bitch," he began. Sameera disconnected the call, but he called back before she could put her phone away.

"Yes?"

"Don't make me come looking for you."

Sameera wasn't afraid of Raja and felt a bit cocky after her conversation with Rhino.

"I dare you to." She disconnected the call and blocked his number. Raja wouldn't dare come to Dallas; if he did, he would be in for a surprise.

Chapter Thirty-Four

Valentine's Day

~Sameera~

Sameera had been so tired from her training the day before that when she got home, she ate, soaked in the tub, and while watching a movie with Hippo, she fell asleep beside him on the sofa. Her sister had gone upstairs to give them some time alone. Sameera hadn't told her about Raja's call. She didn't expect him to figure out where they were, so there was no point in bringing it up.

Opening her eyes, she was tucked into Hippo's side with his good arm around her. They were still on the sofa. She raised her head to look at him. He looked like he was still sleeping. Sameera smiled, laying her head back against his chest. She listened to his heartbeat, sniffing his scent. He smelled good, natural, with just a hint of cologne.

She didn't want to get up, but she had to. She had been so tired after training that she decided to come straight home instead of going out to find something to wear for their Valentine's date. Since Mike had canceled their training because of the holiday, Sameera could go shopping today. She would take Haimari to get something for her date with Panther. She tried to get up without waking Hippo, but as soon as she had thrown her leg over his to get up, he opened his eyes. She smiled at him.

"Sorry, I was trying to get up without waking you."

He tightened his arm, bringing her body flush against his. She made sure that she wasn't putting any pressure on his broken leg as he kissed her cheek.

"I know, but I've been awake for a while," he told her when she looked into his eyes.

He shifted his shoulder. "Shit," she exclaimed, getting to her feet. "This couldn't have been comfortable for you." She hadn't thought about his collarbone.

He sat up. "It wasn't the best position to be in, but I wasn't in much pain."

"Do you need a pain pill?" She asked, moving to go to his room for them.

"No. I'm good," he said, stopping her. "Do we have time for breakfast before you go to training?"

"I don't have training today. Mike and Warthog gave me the day off. I was going to take Haimari shopping for her date with Panther tonight. I'm sure she's tired of borrowing my clothes, so I figured it would be a good day to let her pick up some things for herself."

"So, you two are awake?" Haimari said as she entered the room. "I came down an hour ago, and you both were sleeping like you were dead."

They all laughed. "I was just telling Kenny that I'm taking you shopping so that you can get something to wear for your date."

Haimari smiled, "Great, because I've been looking at your clothes for the last hour, and nothing seems right for me."

Sameera rolled her eyes. "Whatever."

"Go get dressed. I'll make everyone some coffee."

181

Chapter Thirty-Five

~Hippo~

After Sameera left the room, Hippo maneuvered into his wheelchair and went to his room. He grabbed his wallet and took out a credit card, returning to the kitchen.

"Here," he said, handing it to Haimari. "I know Sameera won't take it if I try to give it to her. Your shopping trip is on me, got it? Don't let her pay for anything."

Haimari took the card from him. "Alright. Am I allowed to tell her? What about what you bought yesterday."

He thought about it for a minute. "Sure, you can tell her it is my treat, but make sure that she understands this is part of my Valentine's Day present to you both."

"Got it."

"Thank you for your help with my surprise for her."

"You're welcome," she said, handing him a mug of coffee just as the doorbell rang. "I'll get it," she told him as she left the room.

"Well, you must be Haimari, Sameera's sister," his mother said after the door was open.

"Come in," Haimari said.

A few seconds later, his mother entered the kitchen with a large glass dish, followed by Haimari. "Hi there," she said, kissing his cheek. "I brought you all some lunch."

"What is it?" Hippo asked.

"Lasagna," she said, moving around him to put it in the fridge. "All you have to do is stick it in the oven till it's warm."

"Thank you, mom."

She closed the door and set her purse on the counter, looking at Haimari. "You're as pretty as your sister."

Haimari smiled, "Thank you, Ma'am."

"Call me Dottie. Where is Sameera?"

"I'm right here," Sameera said from the doorway. His mother crossed the room and hugged her.

"I'm going to go clean up a bit. Excuse me," Hippo said as he realized he hadn't brushed his teeth or washed his face. The women stepped aside so that he could get past them.

He listened to them laughing and talking as he went to his room. It felt like a home for the first time since he bought the house, all because of Sameera. She was changing his life, and he liked it.

He didn't mean to compare her to Cougar, but he couldn't help but see their differences. Cougar and Sameera were both beautiful and strong women, but they were very different individuals. He'd never felt that his feelings were reciprocated with Cougar. She kept him at arm's length, where Sameera opened him up to what could be. He thought he loved Cougar, but he was sure of his feelings about Sameera. *I love her.*

He wasn't just falling in love. It was a fact. He loved her for who she was. *My Sammi is sweet and kind. She thinks of others before thinking of herself. She's beautiful physically, and I can't wait to learn more about her.* He wanted to dance around shouting about his feelings but restrained himself for more reasons than his bum leg. He knew how he felt but didn't believe Sameera was in the same place yet. He would give her the time she needed. Then they could celebrate their feelings together.

~Claudia~

The prepaid phone she purchased at Target danced across the table. Her husband was the only one who had the number. This was the third time this morning that he tried to reach her. Her kids had stopped playing and were looking at her to see what she would do.

She wanted to answer it, to tell him that she was okay, but she wasn't ready to speak to him again. He would try to talk her out of running, and she couldn't do that. Claudia was also still upset with Harrison. If he hadn't gotten them into this mess in the first place, she wouldn't have had to hide for the rest of her life. She also wouldn't have Kyle.

When the phone stopped ringing, the boys returned to playing with the toys she had packed for them. Claudia needed to think of somewhere to go. She knew that they couldn't stay at the ranch. Sooner or later, Harrison would figure out that's where she had gone. She didn't want to be here when the police arrived to get her. *We'll stay one more night. In the morning, we'll get on the road, and I'll find a place for us to go.*

~Harrison~

"She's not answering," Harrison told the people who were protecting him and trying to locate his wife.

"Alright, we'll give it a break for now," Puma said as he handed the man another cup of coffee. "Mr. Bunker, where would your wife go?"

"I don't know."

"Family? Friends?"

186

"She wouldn't go to any of her friends. Claudia wouldn't want to put them in danger. As for family," he said, sighing heavily, "We don't really have any. My parents have been dead for a while. Her mother died over ten years ago. Her father –" he paused briefly, remembering the property that his father had when he died. "He died recently. So there is no one that she would go to." He should have told the truth, but he couldn't do it. He knew that Claudia would come to her senses eventually. She wasn't built for a life on the run. They were both nearly sixty. Just handling the boys daily was almost too much for her. He knew he could talk her out of this madness if only she would answer the phone.

~Goose~

He was late getting to the shop on Valentine's Day because he stopped to get a gift for Cherie and Gazelle. As far as he knew, neither woman was involved with anyone. He understood what it was like watching everyone around you getting gifts and making plans with the one they loved. He and his brother were both single. Although Moose seemed to have a few ladies in his life, he wasn't seriously involved with any of them. In fact, he didn't even bother to do anything to celebrate the holiday.

Cherie wasn't behind the counter when he entered. She was adjusting some things in the clothing area. She looked up as the chime sounded.

"Morning."

Goose returned her greeting. "Good morning, and Happy Valentine's Day," he said, handing her a small white box.

"What's this?"

"A gift for you." The look she gave him conveyed her embarrassment. "Open it," he said as she took it from him.

"I – I don't have anything for you."

"It's okay. I just picked this up on the way in." He watched as she lifted the lid. Once she saw what was in the box, she smiled.

"It's strawberry," he told her. "I hope that's okay.

Cherie lifted the cupcake from the box, flicking her tongue out to taste the pink frosting. "It's perfect," she said after her taste test. "Thank you."

Goose pushed away the dirty thoughts that flashed in his head of her licking that frosting from his body. "You're welcome," he said, moving towards the workroom door. He stopped, turning back to her. "If you need to leave early, let me know."

"Why would I need to leave early?" She questioned before she bit into the cupcake.

"You know, in case you have a date for tonight and need to get ready."

Cherie almost choked on her food. She finished what was in her mouth. "Yeah – uh, I don't have any plans, but thanks for considering it."

He smiled and went through the door. *No date means no boyfriend. I could ask her out, but what if she does have a boyfriend, and he's out of town or something.* He shook his head and went to where Gazelle was sitting.

"Happy Valentine's Day," he said, handing her the muffin he had for her. It was like the one he'd given Cherie, but it was blueberry. It seemed to be her favorite flavor whenever he or Moose brought a mixed box from the Bakery down the road.

"Thanks," she said without looking up.

She hardly ever smiled and always seemed serious, but today she seemed more apathetic than usual. "Everything okay?" He asked.

She looked at him and sighed. "Yeah, I'm just having a hard time with the woman who runs the boarding house where I rent a room."

"What kind of trouble?"

"Nothing serious. She has been trying to introduce me to some men since I've been there, and I finally told her I'm gay. Now she's trying to fix me up with women. It's annoying, but I'm looking for a new place to live."

"Sorry to hear that. Are you looking for anything in particular?"

"No. I just want to find something that's nice and not too expensive."

"Are we not paying you enough?"

"Oh God, I wasn't trying to insinuate that I need a raise or anything. What you're paying me is great. I just have some debt I'm trying to handle, so I have to budget carefully."

"Oh, okay. If I can help you find a place, let me know."

"Sure thing," she said, turning away from him and getting back to work.

He had to admit that he didn't know much about Gazelle other than she was gay and awesome with wiring. She was quiet and kept to herself. He moved away from her to his own area. He had a lot to do, and it wouldn't get done on its own.

Chapter Thirty-Six

~Sameera~

Spending the day with Haimari preparing for their Valentine's dates was a lot of fun for Sameera. She was completely surprised when Haimari pulled out her wallet and told her that Kenny insisted everything be put on his card.

After choosing their clothing, they shopped at several stores to buy shoes and accessories. They had a quick meal in the mall food concourse before going into one of the salons to have their hair and nails done.

When they got back to the house, all was quiet. Dottie's car was gone from the driveway, and Kenny must have been in his room. Sameera wanted to go and thank him for funding their outing, but first, they took their purchases up to the bedroom.

Sameera noticed a large gift box on the bed as she stepped into the room. "What's that?"

"It's for you." Haimari moved to the other side of the bed, putting her shopping bags on the floor. Sameera sat hers by the closet door. "How do you know it's for me?"

"Yesterday, Kenny and I went shopping for you. It's his Valentine's Day gift."

"Really?"

"Open it," Haimari said, sitting on the edge of the bed.

Sameera grinned as she lifted the lid and pulled the tissue back. "Oh," she said, looking at the beautiful coral-colored strapless dress inside. She didn't miss the matching high-heeled shoes tucked into the corner. "And shoes too?" She questioned, looking at her sister.

"There's more," Hairmari offered.

Lifting the dress out of the box, she discovered a small box under it. Sameera laid the dress out beside the large gift box before removing the shoes and placing them on the bed with the dress. Then she picked up the smaller box to open. Inside was a double-heart diamond pendant necklace with matching earrings and a bracelet.

"Wow. They're beautiful."

"The man's got great taste," Haimari said, getting up. "We have enough time to relax for a bit, and I think you should take a nap."

Sameera agreed with her. Even though she had gotten at least six hours of sleep, she was still tired from her workout and training the day before.

"You're right. I want to be well-rested for tonight. If you went shopping for this yesterday, why didn't you mention it while we were shopping today? I didn't need to buy the dress I got today."

Haimari smiled, "Because it would have ruined the surprise. Besides, it's not like you can't wear the dress you picked on some other date with him."

Her sister was right. She moved the jewelry to the dresser top and her dress and shoes to the closet. Once the bed was cleared, she grabbed her phone and texted Gopher to ensure everything she had planned was in place. She got a response back quickly. "Are you going to take a nap too?" She asked Haimari.

"Doubtful. I think I'll keep reading the hot romance I started yesterday, but I'll go downstairs."

Haimari grabbed the book from beside the bed and left the room. Before Sameera lay down, she returned to the dresser and picked up the necklace. It was very pretty and extremely thoughtful. She was excited about what she planned for later.

Chapter Thirty-Seven

~Panther~

It had been a while since Panther took someone out on Valentine's Day. He hadn't had a long-term relationship in a long time. He wouldn't admit it to anyone but he was a little anxious about his date with Haimari. Besides having a brief conversation when they met, he knew nothing about her. He didn't know if she would like the restaurant he'd chosen. What could he do if she didn't like the food they served? It wasn't like he'd be able to get a reservation anywhere else at the last minute. Most places worth going to would be booked solid.

He checked the clock on the dashboard as he parked in front of Hippo's house. He was a few minutes early, but rather be early than late. He ran his hand over his face, looking at his reflection in the rearview mirror.

"I look good," he said, smiling.

He got out and went to the door ringing the bell. Hippo opened it a few minutes later, backing his chair up to let him inside.

"Hey," he said as he closed the door. Then he took a good look at Hippo. "Even with the cast and sling, you look good?"

Hippo was wearing a nice, navy-colored suit with a white shirt and peachy-colored tie with a matching pocket square. The pantleg on the left side had been cut, leaving the cast exposed, but it had been hemmed and looked like it had been altered just for Hippo.

"Thanks. You don't look so bad yourself. Haimari will be down any minute."

"What are you and Sameera doing tonight?"

"I don't know. She planned the date and refused to tell me anything other than we were going out."

"That's interesting."

"What about you?"

"I'm taking Haimari to dinner at SanSaree."

"Nice," Hippo commented just as Haimari entered the entry from the stairs. They both turned.

197

Panther's mouth was suddenly dry. "You look amazing," he said, taking her in from head to toe. Her long dark hair fell in waves around her face. Her large amber eyes were highlighted by the smokey eye shadow. Her lips were a dark pink and shiny from the lip gloss she wore that perfectly matched her halter-styled dress and shoes.

"You look very nice, too," she said, smiling brightly.

"Let me help you with your jacket," he said, taking it from her hand. "Ready?" Panther asked when her coat was in place. She nodded.

As they left, Haimari touched Hippo's arm and said, "See you tomorrow."

It threw Panther for a loop. Did she plan to spend the night with him? While he wasn't opposed to the idea, he hadn't planned to do anything more than have dinner and go dancing.

~Hippo~

Panther and Haimari had only been gone for a few minutes when Sameera came down the stairs. Hippo could hardly breathe, watching her. She looked incredible in the dress he'd chosen for her. The first time he saw her, she was wearing a similar color, and he had noted how it looked against her caramel-colored skin. She was wearing her hair up with a few tendrils hanging loose around her perfectly made face.

The dress was strapless and outlined her curvaceous figure. Luckily he and Haimari were able to find shoes in almost the exact same color. He smiled. "You are so beautiful."

Her smile was sweet as she stopped in front of him. She held out her arms and spun around so that he could get a good look. "Thank you. I wasn't expecting anything like this. I love everything."

"Good because it looks great on you." The doorbell rang.

"That should be our car service," Sameera said, sliding her arms into her coat as she went to the door. She opened it, and a tall blond man stood in a black suit.

"Ms. Bhatt, my name is Ian, and I'll be your driver."

"Thank you," she said to him. She opened the door wider, looking at Hippo. "Are you ready?"

He'd never been more ready for a date in his life. "Yes."

"You rented a limo?" He asked as the driver opened the back door. After he allowed Sameera to get in, Ian assisted Hippo and then put the chair in the trunk. While they waited, he took her hand. "Sammi, no one has ever done anything like this for me. Thank you."

She smiled, squeezing his hand. "I've never done this for anyone, but you're worth the effort."

"Where are we going?"

She shook her head. "You'll see soon enough."

~Sameera~

During the ride to their destination, Sameera tried to the butterflies swirling around her insides. Hippo was so handsome, even with his sling and cast, and he smelled wonderful. Their driver had put the partition up so they could have privacy along the way.

Soft romantic music played in the background. Hippo raised her hand, bringing it to his lips. She held her breath as he placed a few kisses on her skin. Goosebumps popped up along her arm, and the butterflies flew as tingles raced from her hand through her body. She was happy and nervous about her gift to him. She would give it to him later after dinner.

By the time they arrived, the sun was gone from the sky. She giggled as Kenny tried to see out the window. Ian opened her door, got the wheelchair out of the trunk, and brought it to the other side of the car.

Once Hippo was seated, Ian handed her a card. "Just call me when you're ready to return home, and I'll be here to get you in half an hour."

"Thank you," she said to him.

She watched Kenny as he looked at the dock. "We're going out in a yacht?" He asked, grinning as he looked up at her. "How on earth-" he began to ask, but Sameera interrupted him.

"Gopher, of course. I called him last week and asked if he could help me find an affordable night cruise, which he found."

"It has to be at least a few hundred feet long," Hippo said, staring at its length.

"Three hundred and eighty-five feet, to be exact, and all he would tell me was that it belongs to someone he knows."

Hippo stared at her. "That's longer than a football field, and it's the most anyone has ever gotten out of him. He always tells us not to ask how he can get the things he does."

"Must be my charm," Sameera said with a smile. "Come on, let's check this thing out."

~Hippo~

He was assisted from the dock to the yacht by a couple of gentlemen who greeted them at the gangplank.

"Welcome aboard, Mr. Thompson, Ms. Bhatt. I'm Captain Mauberg." Once they were on board, he told them the plan. "We'll cruise halfway around the lake and anchor offshore for the night. We'll cruise around the other half in the morning before we return you to the dock. I'd like you to meet Lana Danvers, the butler. She will see to your needs and enjoyment."

"It's a pleasure to serve you," the dark-haired woman in the white uniform said as the captain left them. "Please come with me, and I'll take you on a brief tour." She turned, and they followed, listening as she explained that they had everything set up on the main deck. "When Mr. Winthrop explained that you would need some special accommodation, we put you in the stateroom on this level. Just let me know if there is anything we didn't account for."

Hippo couldn't believe what he was seeing. The main deck housed a bar, dining room, movie theater, four bedrooms with private baths, and much more. It didn't slip past him that this date lasted until they returned to the dock the next morning. *Maybe that's what Haimari meant when she said she would see me tomorrow.*

When the tour ended, Ms. Danvers took them into the dining room. In the center was a larger-than-average table, set for two. She assisted Sameera with her chair while he could roll up to his place since the chair had been removed. "We have an excellent menu for you tonight. In the four courses we have planned, you will get to experience the chef's finest dishes. Starting with stuffed cremini mushrooms. Then for your second course, you can choose either the Mediterranean salad or the creamy ham and potato soup. We'll serve seared scallops with brown butter and lemon pan sauce or grilled coconut shrimp with shishito peppers for the main course. Finally, we offer the best dessert you will ever experience, chocolate lasagna." Hippo's mouth watered at the thought of it.

A few seconds later, more staff appeared with their first course. They were served, and wine was poured for them. Hippo sat there for a minute, just shaking his head.

"What's wrong?" Sameera asked.

"Nothing. It's perfect." He smiled. His heart was filled with excitement. No one had ever done anything like this for him. His heart was so full of emotion that he feared it might burst out of his chest.

Chapter Thirty-Eight

~Sameera~

The meal was delicious, and the dessert was worth Ms. Danvers's praise. When they left the dining room, they went out on the deck. Hippo gave Sameera his jacket to keep her warm in the cool breeze.

"This has been the best evening," he told her as he took hold of her hand.

"I'm glad that you're enjoying it."

"Does your family own a yacht like this?"

Sameera smiled and looked at the city's twinkling lights beyond the water. "My parents have a yacht, but it's not like this."

She knew he was watching her and could hear the longing in her voice. "I miss them."

"You should contact them and try to put the past behind you. I didn't realize how much I missed my mother until we reunited. If it weren't for you, we might have gone years without reconciling."

"I would love to, but I don't think it's a good idea."

Hippo tugged her hand, making her look at him. He patted his thighs. "Sit," he commanded.

"Are you sure? I don't want to hurt you."

"I'll be fine," he said, pulling her toward him. She gingerly sat down. He wrapped his arms around her. "I like this. You feel like you belong here in my arms."

"I like it too." She turned her torso, meeting his lips with her own. He still tasted like their dessert, chocolatey and sweet.

~Hippo~

They sat on the deck, making out for a while, and the kisses grew more intense. He tried to keep his libido in check, but with each moan she made, he lost a little bit more of his control. It wouldn't be long before she knew it too. His erection was growing quickly. He pulled his mouth from hers. "I think we should go inside. It's too cool out here."

Sameera giggled. "I think it's getting hot if you know what I mean."

He did, and that's why they needed to go inside. It was bad enough that his dick was rock-hard. If they kept kissing, he might explode and embarrass them both. "I do."

Sameera stood up. "I think it's time for me to give you your gift."

He grinned at her. "I thought this date; the yacht and the limo ride were my gifts."

"No. I have something else I want to give you, but we have to go inside."

"Okay. Lead the way, beautiful."

Hippo followed her back to the area where the private cabin bedrooms were. She opened the door and waited for him to enter. His mouth fell open. Rose petals were strewn around the room and on the enormous bed. From where he sat at the foot of the bed, he could see a bottle of champagne and two glasses sitting beside the bottle. As the door closed, Hippo turned his chair to face Sameera. "This is very romantic."

She moved around him, taking his jacket off and laying it on one of the chairs before returning to him. She leaned over him. She was close, but not close enough for him to kiss her lips. He was so focused on her proximity that he didn't realize what she was doing. His tie was loose, and she removed it, tossing it to where his jacket was. "Sameera," he said as she began to unbutton his shirt.

"Yes?"

"You better be sure that you want to do this."

"I'm positive," she replied as she reached the last button where his shirt disappeared into his slacks. Without a moment's hesitation, she began to undo his pants. She was smiling the entire time. He held his breath while she unzipped his pants. Then she removed his shoe and sock, putting them aside. She stood and turned away from him. "Can you help with the zipper?"

Hippo licked his lips and reached up, pulling the zipper down with his good hand. The sneak peek of her black lace underwear made his mouth water. Sameera turned to face him, holding the dress in place. She removed the pins holding her hair up, letting it fall around her shoulders. His breath hitched at the vision of loveliness in front of him.

Sameera smiled and let the dress fall to the floor around her feet. Hippo inhaled deeply, swallowing the lump in his throat. The double heart necklace lay perfectly between the cleft of her bosom. She stood before him in a strapless corset thing that stopped at her waist. Just below it was a garter belt connected over lacey panties to stockings that stopped at the top of her thighs. He snapped several mental pictures to save for later.

"In case you haven't figured it out yet. I'm your gift."

He didn't know what to say. He wanted his gift in the worst way, but he also wanted to make sure she knew he was willing to wait for her. "We don't have to do this just because it's a day for lovers."

"That's exactly why I want this. I want you to be my lover, Kenny." His resolve was weakening quickly. She kissed him, taking his mouth with intention. Sameera was seducing him, and he liked every bit of it. The only thing that bothered him was that he couldn't pick her up and sit her down, so she straddled him in the chair.

When she released his mouth, he said, "I need out of this chair right now." Sameera moved back, allowing him to turn the chair to get around to the side of the bed. When he stood up, she moved the chair out of his way. His pants slid down his legs.

"Sit," she ordered, bending over to remove them before she put them with his jacket. Then she helped him out of his shirt. He had no idea how this would work with one arm in a sling and a leg in a cast, but they could figure it out.

Sameera came back to him, pushing his legs apart to stand between them. "Take that off," he said, staring at her corset. She reached behind her, and a few seconds later, Sameera tossed it aside. Hippo kissed the skin at the top of her tummy, inhaling the light floral scent of her perfume. She quivered and exhaled. Then he kissed the skin between her breasts, working his way across the soft mound until he could close his lips around the erect peak of it. He groaned, and she moaned at the same time.

Hippo took his time sucking and nibbling on one before working his way to the other breast to give it the same love and attention. Her hands cupped the back of his head. He opened his eyes, looking up at her. She watched him enjoy himself, and if he thought he could get harder than he already was, he was wrong.

He took his mouth from her breast, grabbing her at the back of the neck. He pulled her down, taking her mouth and plundering her lips. He never wanted anything as much as he wanted her at that moment, but he had to remind himself that she was new to this, and needed to be gentle with her.

When he let her go, she undid the straps holding the stockings in place. "Leave them and the garter on," he told her. She bit her lip and removed the panties, putting the straps back in place. Hippo dipped his head and let his tongue swipe over her hairless mound. Goosebumps rose on her skin as she shivered.

"I want to taste you," he whispered. "I'm going to lay back, and you need to position yourself above me so I can pleasure you with my mouth, okay?" She bit her lip and nodded quickly.

Once he was in place, she carefully moved over him, ensuring she did not touch his hurt shoulder. "Spread your legs a bit more," he instructed. It brought her down to just the right height. Hippo flicked his tongue over her clit a few times before latching on.

"Oh God," Sameera grunted, arching her back.

Hippo placed his free hand on her hip to bring her back to the right spot where he could easily access her nub. Then he moved his hand to her opening, using his fingers to test her slickness. She moaned and began working her hips, grinding against his tongue, helping him to bring her to her first climax.

When he realized she was climaxing, he sucked her clit harder, wanting to prolong the sensations she was experiencing. When she began to settle down, her juices dripped down his chin. Hippo ran his tongue along her slit, lapping up her juices. He turned his head, kissing her thighs before scooting from under her. She stayed where she was for a few seconds breathing hard. He liked the view from where he lay. "You okay?"

"Mmmhmm," she moaned with her face buried in the blanket. She carefully turned over, grabbing a pillow to hold in front of her.

"Don't be embarrassed." Her cheeks were flushed with color, her hair was wild and messy. He loved how she looked.

"I had no idea it would feel that good," she said, trying not to smile.

"That was nothing," Hippo said, grinning.

Sameera scooted off the bed and grabbed his underwear. He lifted his hips as best as possible to help her remove them. When his dick sprang free, Sameera gasped. "It's so big."

Hippo couldn't help the laughter from him as he raised his head to see her. She was staring at his dick with such awe that he flexed his pelvic muscle, causing it to move.

"Oh, my God!" He laughed, and she smiled, looking him in the face. "Do it again." He did, and when it was standing upright, she grabbed it, tossing his underpants away.

Hippo groaned. Her hand was warm as she tried to get her hand around it. Before he realized what she intended, she ran her tongue from the base to the tip. Hippo tightened his stomach muscles and inhaled.

"Careful," he warned her. She did it again. He grabbed her by the hair, pulling her towards him. When they lay chest to chest, he looked her in the eye. "You're not ready for that yet."

She pouted. "I just wanted to do to you what you did to me."

"Not yet, okay?" He flexed more, allowing his dick to rub against her slick opening. "This is your first time, and I don't want to do that because it would be more about my pleasure than yours."

Sameera had started to wiggle her hips, rubbing herself against him. She kissed him slowly, passionately. Hippo took hold of himself and rubbed her easing himself into her slowly. She wiggled her hips as he worked a bit more of himself inside her. She released his lips, biting hers. "This could be painful for you. Take it slowly, a little at a time," he warned.

He could tell when he broke through. She winced and stopped moving. "Relax, baby. Let your body adjust." He ran his hand up and down her back. Then he moved again, sliding out a little and then further in. Sameera's eyes closed, and she began to rock in tempo with him. "You okay?" She nodded her head.

They continued that way for a while. Hippo waited for her cue that she wanted more. When she moved faster, he did too. Sameera opened her eyes to find him watching her. She smiled and leaned down, kissing him. He picked up his tempo, holding her at the back of her neck with his left hand while he worked his hips. Their movements were small thrusts, but it didn't take long for Sameera to near her peak. She moaned into his mouth before tearing her lips from his. "Oh, oh, yes."

Hippo slid his hand down, wrapping it around her waist tightly, holding her in place as he thrust harder and faster into her as he got close to release. He watched her as she came undone in his arms. Then, with a few more powerful thrusts, he let go and realized that they hadn't used a condom.

He closed his eyes, angry at himself for not thinking of it. There was so much they hadn't talked about yet. He didn't know if she wanted children. What if she didn't, and she ended up pregnant?

They lay there for a few minutes. He stroked her back, loving the feel of her skin. He didn't want to ruin what they had just experienced together. They could have the baby conversation in the morning.

She raised her head. "How's your collarbone?"

He smiled lazily at her. "It's fine." She eased off of him, getting up. "Where are you going?"

"Be right back," she said, going through the door that led to the bathroom. She returned with a couple of towels. She used the small damp washrag to clean him up. Then she dried his skin with the other.

"Thank you," he told her as she left the room.

"I'm going to clean up, and then I'll come to bed," she called out as she closed the door.

Chapter Thirty-Nine

~Sameera~

When she woke, Sameera was alone in bed. Smiling, she grabbed his pillow and breathed in the scent of him.

Last night when she returned to find to the bedroom she found Kenny under the covers dozing. Sameera got in on the other side. She turned out the lights and snuggled in the bed, leaving room between them in case he needed it. She had barely gotten comfortable before he turned over, spooning her. He kissed her shoulder.

Before he could fall asleep again, she asked, "Do you need a pain pill?"

"You are all I need," he said, pulling her back tighter against his chest.

They fell asleep like that.

As she remembered the feel of his lips, hands, and other parts on and in her body, she wondered where he was. She sat up, looking around the room.

His clothes were gone, and hers were neatly lying on the back of one of the large chairs on the other side of the room.

Sameera got out of bed and checked the time. They should be heading back by now. She used the bathroom and cleaned herself up. She didn't bother to put her hair back up. She combed it with her fingers and left the cabin to find Kenny.

He was sitting where they had been last night at the back of the yacht.

"Good morning," she said near his ear as she reached him.

"Morning," he said as he turned his head towards her. He kissed her briefly.

"Have you been up long?"

"For about an hour."

"Why didn't you wake me?"

"Because if I had, I wouldn't have been able to keep my hands off you."

That made her smile. "Next time, wake me up."

He chuckled, "Your body needs time, plus I was thinking."

"About what?"

Hippo raised his head to look at her. "We didn't use a condom last night. It was irresponsible of me. We haven't talked about children, and this is so new that I don't want you to regret any of it."

Sameera moved around him so that she could look directly at him. "Kenny, I had condoms in my purse."

"What? Why didn't you say something last night?"

Sameera sighed and shoved the hair from her face as the wind picked up. "I never considered life with a husband or children until I met this guy who makes my heart race. He's kind and handsome. He is protective and sweet and sexy as hell. That's when I saw myself having a family and children with his features."

"Who is this guy? Do I know him?" Hippo joked.

"If what we share creates a new life, I'd be thrilled about it."

"You would?"

"Yeah. Would it be better if we waited? Maybe, maybe not. This is new, and last night we both got caught up in an intensely emotional, physical connection. Still, I will never regret it, no matter what happens." She was quiet for a minute, looking away from him. "Would it be a problem for you if I did get pregnant last night?"

He smiled, shaking his head. "No. I love you, Sammi."

Her heart flipped in her chest. "You love me?"

"Yes," he said, taking her hand.

She smiled as a tear rolled down her cheek. She pressed her lips together, taking a deep breath. "I love you too, Kenny."

Hippo pulled her close, kissing her. Then with their foreheads pressed together, they grinned at each other.

When they were docked, the captain met them at the ramp. "I hope you enjoyed your voyage on the Don't Ask, Don't Tell."

"Excuse me," Hippo said. "Is that the name of the boat?"

"Yes, sir," the captain replied with a nod of his head.

"Do you and your crew regularly work on this yacht?"

"Yes, sir."

"Who's the owner?"

"I'm not a liberty to divulge that information."

Hippo grinned, shaking his head. It was too much of a coincidence that Gopher arranged the yacht and always replied to questions about how he could supply everything they needed with 'don't ask.'

"Thank you. We had a lovely time," Sameera said to the captain as they got off the boat. Ian was waiting for them when they got to the parking area. They got in, cuddling as he took them home.

~Claudia~

Her plans to leave the ranch when they got up changed as soon as she got the children. Daniel was not well. He had coughed a few times before she put them to bed, but when he woke congested with a fever, Claudia decided that she didn't want to be on the road with him feeling bad. It was mid-afternoon, and now Kyle was sniffling too.

She tended to them, keeping them in bed. There was no cable or internet in the house. Still, she had thought to bring some of their favorite books, and thankfully when she grabbed things out of the bathroom, Claudia put the cold medicine in the bag too.

She soothed them both, reading to them, Kyle was still energetic enough to play by himself, but at the rate that she was cleaning his nose, it was only a matter of time before he would be in bed with whatever it was that Daniel had caught.

She planned to contact Harrison when she got far enough away from the ranch to feel safe, but whenever the boys were ill, Harrison would cuddle with them and tell them stories. It made them feel better. They had been asking for him, and she didn't know what else to do.

She picked up the phone, holding it to her chest for a few seconds. Then she dialed his number. He picked it up on the first ring.

"Hello, Claudia?"

"Harrison, the boys are sick. They've caught a cold or something. They've been asking for you. Will you talk to them, tell them a story?"

"Of course, put them on," her husband said without hesitation.

Claudia put the call on speaker and sat on the bed with them. "Your dad is on the phone," she told them. They both smiled and began talking to him.

~Rabbit~

When the cloned phone rang, Rabbit picked it up and listened to the conversation between Harrison and his wife. She began trying to trace the call immediately. If they stayed on the line long enough, she could get an idea of where Mrs. Bunker was.

Puma had told her that Harrison had attempted to call her several times the day before. It didn't surprise her when her own phone buzzed with a text from him that Harrison was on the phone with her.

She quickly sent a message that she was trying to get a location on her. She didn't think that Harrison and Claudia were bad people. They were simply parents that loved their kid and didn't want to lose him.

He talked to them lovingly, telling them a story about a squirrel that became friends with a duck. It was a cute story that tugged at her heart while she watched the first indicator pop up on her screen. Claudia was still in Texas. *I hope this story is long enough to get two more markers on the map.*

When he finished the story, Harrison's wife talked to him again.

"Honey, please tell me where you are?"

"I can't," she said softly.

"We can't keep him. It's time for him to be with his mother. She deserves to know that he's alive and well. Put yourself in her shoes."

"I have." There was a short pause. "I love him too much to just hand him over. I'm the one he calls mommy. I'm the one who has taken care of him and loved him since you brought him home."

"I know, but we have to do what's right for him and her."

The second marker popped up on Rabbit's screen. *Just a little while longer. Keep her talking just a minute or two longer, Harrison.* Rabbit kept her eyes on the screen and prayed that this would work.

"I just – I don't want to be without him."

"Maybe his mother will allow you to see him, keep in touch."

"Why would she do that? As far as she's concerned, we stole her child from her."

"You didn't steal him. You gave him a home, love, and care. She will appreciate you doing that."

The third marker appeared, and Rabbit shouted, "Yes!" She quickly texted Mike and Cougar that she had a general location. A few seconds later, she got a text from Mike that they were calling the available Beasts in to get organized and for her to meet them in half an hour at the clubhouse. Harrison and Claudia were still talking.

"It won't matter. As soon as the boys feel better, I will take them somewhere no one can find us. I love you, but I'm not giving him up." She disconnected the call. Rabbit printed the image on her screen. She moved quickly to get her things together and leave her apartment.

Chapter Forty

~Cougar~

As soon as she got Rabbit's message, Cougar pulled over and texted all The Beasts that they finally had a location to search for Claudia and to come to the clubhouse to organize the search party. She also sent a separate message to Diego not to tell Harrison.

She wanted to find his wife and the baby without any possible interference from him. He wanted to do the right thing, but he also loved his wife and their children. It was possible he might have a change of heart and warn his wife that they were coming. Once she was finished texting, Cougar got back on the road, heading to the clubhouse.

It only took her a few minutes to get there. Mike, Rhino, and a few others were already upstairs when she arrived.

"Have you talked to Rabbit?" She asked Mike.

"She's on her way," Mike told her.

"Good."

Within fifteen minutes, more of the club members entered and took a seat around the table. Rabbit came rushing in, waving a sheet of paper at Mike and Cougar. "She's in Central Texas." She pointed to the map.

Mike took it from her hand. "That's a big area."

"Yeah, give me a few minutes to see if I can get a shot from Google Maps that might narrow our search," Rabbit told him as she moved away to set up her computer on the conference table.

"We have to be very careful going in to get them. I don't think she will be a problem, but she's a mother trying not to lose her kid. We can't have anything happen to the children. This is all going to be traumatic enough for them."

"I agree," Mike said. "Have we asked Harrison if they had any weapons she might have taken with her?"

"Diego has talked to him more than anyone over the past few days. I'll call and ask him," Cougar said, taking out her phone.

~Hippo~

The car slowed down. Hippo opened his eyes, checking their location. They were nearly home. Sameera's eyes were closed, and she was lost in ecstasy as she rolled her hips. "Yes, yes."

He didn't intend for them to have sex on the way back to his house, but kissing led to touching, and before he knew it, she had climbed onto his lap and was giving him the ride of his life. He knew he had to help her along, or Ian would be in for a surprise when he parked the car.

Hippo slid his hand down to her love button and rubbed furiously until she threw her head back as she came undone. He removed his fingers, slid his arm around her waist, and thrust deeply into her a few times, causing his orgasm. Hippo squeezed his eyes shut and grunted, sounding like the animal he was called.

A few more turns, and they would be home. Sameera kissed him, still grinding her hips. He pulled his lips from hers. "Baby, we're almost home," he whispered in her ear.

She nodded her head and slowly slid off his lap. He gave her his pocket square to wipe away the evidence. She smiled at him, and when she was finished, she tucked his man bits away and grinned as she slid his hanky back into his pocket. "Thanks for the ride," she said, pushing the skirt of her dress in place and sitting beside him just as the car stopped in front of their house.

Ian opened the door for Sameera after he got Hippo's chair from the trunk. Once he was in his chair, she stood beside him, holding Hippo's hand. "Ian, thank you so much for giving us the most enjoyable ride."

Hippo couldn't help but snicker at her comment and its double meaning.

"It was my pleasure," Ian replied. "You have my card if you ever need my services again.

No, dude. It was MY pleasure. Hippo grinned as the man walked back to the driver's side of the limo.

~Sameera~

As they entered the house, her phone chirped at the same time that Hippo's went off. That could only be a message pertaining to the club. They both checked their messages as she closed the door. "They've found Michelle's kid," Kenny said.

While happy about that, she wasn't ready to be apart from Kenny. "I better get showered and get to the clubhouse."

"I don't want you to go." His lip was poked out like a little kid.

Sameera bent down, kissing him. "I don't want to go, but they might need me."

"Okay, just be careful."

"Always," she said, moving around him to climb the stairs.

When she entered the bedroom, Haimari was sitting in the center of the bed with a book in her hands. "Well, how did it go?"

Sameera rushed past her, pulling open drawers and removing what she needed. "I'll have to tell you later. I have to get to the clubhouse. They found the kid we've been looking for. I need to shower and change."

"Did you two hump like camels or what?" Haimari asked as Sameera rushed towards the bathroom. She stopped at the door, turning to look at her sister. She closed her eyes briefly, smiling as she thought of how wonderful things had turned out last night and in the limo. "You did!" Haimari exclaimed.

"It was – magical," Sameera said, entering the bathroom and closing the door.

"We'll talk about this when you get back," Haimari shouted.

Sameera had no idea that while washing her body, she would have flashbacks of Kenny's hands on her. It was like he had brought her into a new state of being. Everything was sensitive. She ignored it as much as she could and hurried along.

She dressed in Jeans and a long-sleeved tee shirt, pulled her still-wet hair into a ponytail, rushing from the bathroom to put on socks and sneakers. Haimari watched her moving around the room without saying a word.

"I'm not sure when I'll be back," she told her sister as she tied the laces on her shoes.

"Is this thing you're going to do dangerous?"

Sameera could hear the concern in her sister's voice. She stood and moved around the bed to where Haimari sat. "It's no more dangerous than anything I've been doing, but I don't think so. Don't worry about me, okay?"

"I can't help it. It worries me a little now that you've explained what you've been up to for the last few years."

Sameera hugged Haimari. "I know you don't know them well, but this group of people would never let anything happen to me. We'll take care of each other. Besides, I have a bigger reason to ensure that I'm careful and return to this house. I have you and Kenny to come home to." She stepped back from her sister. "When I get back, you can tell me about your date with Panther."

"Okay," Hairmari said as Sameera got her jacket from the closet.

"I've got to go," she said, slipping her arms inside her denim jacket.

Sameera jogged down the stairs to Hippo's room. He rolled out of the bathroom, looking damp and sexy. "I thought you might have gone already."

"Not without one more kiss," she said as he stopped in front of her. She leaned down, cupping his face before brushing her lips over his. Already, she could feel the desire building inside her. She pulled back, looking into his beautiful brown eyes. "I love you."

He smiled, pressing his forehead to hers. "I love you more."

She stood up, "I'll be back as soon as I can." She kissed him again and left before she changed her mind.

Chapter Forty-One

~The Beasts~

"Don't worry, we'll bring everyone home safely," Cougar said before disconnecting the call she had been on. She went to Mike, who was leaning over Rabbit's shoulder, looking at her screen. She cleared her throat, causing them both to look in her direction. "I spoke to Amethyst and gave her the information that we have. She and her partner Talia are coming here. They'll go with us so that they can take the kid and get his DNA tested. Thankfully, they got Michelle's DNA sample after we rescued her and the others."

"We need to call Kelly, too," Mike said.

"Done. She'll be waiting to hear from us."

"Okay. Rabbit, let's show everyone what we have." Rabbit put the image from Google maps on the big screen. The Beasts got quiet and began taking seats facing it. "Rabbit was able to determine that Mrs. Bunker is in Flatrock, in Bell county, a few hours north of Austin. It's a pretty rural area with a lot of open terrain. It looks like her father owned some land there, and from this image," he said, looking at Rabbit, who replaced the picture on the screen with a satellite image. "We can see that there is a house there. The deed is in her name, so it's safe to say she's probably there. Gopher has arranged a small plane that will hold ten of us, excluding the pilot. Amethyst and her partner are on their way here, and with me and Cougar, that leaves six seats open. I don't expect to need many of you there, but I want some backup just in case." Sameera came in and stood at the top of the stairs. "Sameera, Panther, Goose, Moose, Bull, and Wolf will accompany us. The rest of you will stay behind. Hopefully, we'll come back without any problems, but keep your phones on in case we need you."

~Sameera~

Sameera crossed the room. "Sorry for being late."

"You're here. That's what matters," Cougar told her.

"Warthog says that you've been doing well with your gun training. I know you don't have a weapon, but I want you to have one, just in case. Come with me."

Mike took her to the back hallway and pulled out a key to a cabinet she had never noticed before. Inside there were rows of weapons. "Which one do you feel comfortable with?"

"The Glock G43XMOS," she said, pointing to one. Mike handed it to her and pulled out a holster that she could attach to the waistband of her jeans. He also handed her a full clip for it. "I hope I won't need this."

"Me too, but better safe than sorry," Mike said as he closed and locked the cabinet. He quickly reviewed the information she missed as they walked back to the group who were going. Amethyst and her partner were speaking with Cougar when they returned to the others. Mike greeted them. "Hey, Am, Thalia."

"Cougar brought us up to speed about where she is and how we're getting there. What's the plan for getting her to come back with us?"

Mike smiled. "I'm hoping that one of you can talk her into it. We'll be there just in case she's taken off already. Gopher will have cars waiting for us at the airstrip where we're landing. If she's already left the house, we'll try to track her down on the ground. Let's get going?"

"Who's the new girl?" Amethyst asked as they walked down the stairs.

Sameera didn't answer since the question was directed at Mike. "She's a new member. We haven't named her yet. Sameera, this is Amethyst and Thalia. They work for the FBI." Amethyst and Thalia both nodded acknowledgments. "She's the one that warned us that Hector sent her to kidnap my niece."

They took two cars. Sameera rode with Panther, sitting in the front with him while Moose, Goose, and Wolf rode in the back. She stared out the window. Her mind was on Hippo and how happy she was instead of being on their mission. She needed to focus on the task at hand. She could think about Hippo when their mission was over.

~Raja~

Raja Gottipotti entered his fiancé's father's study, watching Mahboob as he pulled a large envelope out of his desk drawer. "Thank you for seeing me, Mr. Bhatt. Have you spoken to Haimari?"

The older man sat back in his chair. "I have no reason to speak to her. She left the same as her sister without my permission or blessing."

Raja stood in front of the ornate wooden desk trimmed in gold. "I understand how you must feel, but I believe Haimari will return to her senses if I speak with her."

"I'm not so sure about that, based on what my investigators have witnessed." Before Raja could ask what he meant, Haimari's father tossed the envelope he had taken from the drawer across the desk. "Look for yourself."

Raja picked up the envelope to see what was inside. He pulled out a stack of photos. They were images of Haimari dancing with a tall Black man. She was smiling as if having a good time. There were other pictures of her with her sister coming out of the building in leggings and workout clothes. The final pictures were of Sameera with a man in a wheelchair. All of this was her fault. She had convinced Haimari to leave him.

Mahboob watched the young man before speaking. "My investigator emailed those pictures to me this morning. As you can see, they have both disgraced themselves. The men in those pictures are not the kind of people they should associate with."

"Are you saying that you aren't going to do anything about this?"

"That's exactly what I'm saying. Meera and I tried many times to reign Sameera in, and when we realized it was useless, we stopped trying. Now, she has convinced her sister to follow her to Dallas, Texas, of all places. She has inserted her influence and gotten Haimari to behave just as abominably. We are cutting ties with them both." Raja stuffed the photos into the envelope and returned them to Haimari's father. "I am deeply apologetic about the way this has happened. I hope that you will not place the blame on us for the failed match we tried to make with you and our daughter."

Raja didn't respond. If Mahboob wasn't man enough to control his daughter and return her to complete the marriage contract, he would do it himself. He turned and walked out.

~Hippo~

After Sameera left, Hippo realized even though he wasn't in the kind of pain he had been initially, his collarbone was bothering him. He took a pain pill and laid down. He would nap until he got a call from Sameera or she came home.

When his phone rang, Hippo grabbed it, hoping it was his baby calling to say she would be home soon. "Hello?"

"Kenny, did I wake you?" His mother asked.

He realized that he probably sounded groggy to her. "I was napping, but it's okay. I should get up."

"Well, I called to tell you that when your friends are finished with the repairs to the church, the pastor wants to have a little gathering on Saturday to thank them. I want to make sure that you and Sameera are there. Bring Haimari too."

"Sure. What time should we come?"

"We'll be setting up around two, but the celebration won't start until three."

"Okay. I'll make sure that we're there."

"Great, baby, thank you again for taking care of this."

Hippo could tell that she was trying not to cry. "Momma, I'm glad that we could help."

"Okay, I need to go. Don't forget Saturday at three."

"I won't forget," Hippo said before she hung up.

He checked to make sure he hadn't missed any calls or messages. She hadn't called yet. He had been asleep for a couple of hours. He got up and into his chair. He was hungry.

Haimari was standing in the kitchen at the counter eating. "Hey," he said as he rolled in.

"Hi," she said, holding her hand up to block her mouth.

"What are you munching on?"

Haimari swallowed, dropping her hand. "Some of your mother's lasagna. It is so yummy."

"Mmm, that sounds good."

"I can heat some up for you," she said, getting a plate from the cabinet before he could answer her.

"Thanks. I came in here for that very reason. "I got a call from my mother. We have been invited to a party at her church on Saturday afternoon. The damage to her church will be done, and she wants to thank my club for their hard work."

Haimari put the food in the microwave and started it. "That's nice. Does your club do that kind of thing often?"

"What? Helping the community?" She nodded. "We don't go out looking for community projects, but if we hear about them and can help, we do."

"Maybe the club should have some kind of community outreach program. You could help people with things like what you did for your mother's church. I bet there are a lot of people who have those same kinds of problems. Or you could clean up the neighborhood parks and make sure that the kids have a safe place to play."

Hippo liked the idea. "That's a nice idea, but I don't think anyone of our members has the time to do that kind of thing on a regular basis. Everyone has businesses to run."

The timer beeped on the microwave. Haimari took the food out and put it on the counter near him. "I could run it," she said quietly. "I mean that I could if I stayed here in town."

Hippo smiled. She was uncertain. That was evident. "Is that what you want, to stay in town?"

She looked him in the eye. "I think so. I – feel like I could be useful and do something good. I can't return to New York, even if I wanted to."

"What do you mean?"

"I've tried speaking to my parents several times. Neither of them will answer my calls. I called my father's office, and his secretary told me he was unavailable. I didn't believe her."

"Maybe he was in a meeting or something." It sounded lame to his own ears. "Look, I told you that you could stay here, and I meant it. If you're worried about money, don't be. I may not be rich, but I'm doing alright."

Haimari snorted, "It's not about money. Sammi and I have access to money our parents put into a trust fund for us, but I would like to follow my sister's example and not use it. If I'm going to assert my independence from them, I should learn a skill or get a job."

"Well, what kind of things can you do?"

"I don't know. I haven't done much but help my mother with her charity work."

"Well, it sounds like you would be the person to run this community outreach program you were talking about."

Her eyes widened, and she shook her head. "I've never been in charge. I just do what I'm told."

"It may be time for you to think about how you would organize and run a program like what you described. Tell you what, you think about it. Write down what you would like to do to help the community, then break down what it would take to make it work. When you're ready, we'll take it from there."

She smiled brightly, "I see why my sister wants to stay here. You're good people."

"We try to be, but we all feel like we have committed enough sins that we should try to make amends." He put his plate on his lap now that it had cooled off. "Do you play video games?" She shook her head. "Well, you're going to learn. Grab your plate and follow me to the living room."

Chapter Forty-Two

~The Beasts~

Gopher surprised them when they reached the small airport north of the city. He was going to be their pilot. At first, they thought it was a joke, but everyone realized he was serious when he climbed into the cockpit and fired up the engine.

The flight wasn't bad, though the small confines of the cabin didn't make the ride easier. When they landed, a few guys gave him a hard time. "You couldn't get us a fancy jet with a bar?"

Gopher grinned, taking off his aviator glasses as he got out. "I could have, but I've always wanted to fly one of these."

Cougar shook her head. "It doesn't matter how luxurious the flight could have been. We're here now. Let's get on the road."

Sameera whispered to Panther, "You guys usually fly on private jets for your missions?"

He grinned at her. "Sometimes. You never know what Gopher is going to come up with. But he always provides what we need."

They split into two cars and began the trip to the ranch in Flatrock. Cougar, Mike, Amethyst, and Talia rode in the first car with Sameera.

"Mike, I'm curious about why you picked this particular group of people to make this trip? Sameera asked once they were underway.

"I chose you and Panther because of your lock-picking skills. I picked Wolf because he's an EMT as well as a fireman. Lion had surgery, so he couldn't be here. Bull, Moose, and Goose are here because the D.A. thinks that the Bunkers are targets for whoever is behind the kidnapped women. Bull is a crack shot, and he's good at hand-to-hand combat. Moose and Goose are also good in a fight. They tend to move as if they are one person. Cougar is also a badass. I picked the team that I was sure would be able to handle themselves if we had to get down and dirty. That includes you."

Sameera tried not to smile. "You have that much faith in me?"

"Yes, I do. Was I wrong to include you?"

"No," she said, shaking her head. "I belong here."

The sun was going down by the time they got close to the private road leading to the house. It was far back from the road and surrounded by trees until the house came into view. Then the trees thinned out. A Mercedes station wagon was parked in front of the house, and the lights inside were on.

They parked their vehicles in the trees off the main road. Mike divided them into groups of two and told them how he wanted them to approach the house. "We need to have all sides covered. Keep your weapons holstered. We believe she's in there with just the kids, but keep an eye out for any possible signs of danger. If someone is out here hoping to get to her or the children, we'll handle them while Am and Thalia get in. Sameera and Panther, I want you to keep them in sight until they're inside."

They moved toward the house as quietly as possible. Amethyst and her partner stood on the porch. Everyone had their hands on their guns, ready to draw them if needed. She knocked.

"Mrs. Bunker. My name is Amethyst Woods. I'm with the FBI. Please open the door."

It was quiet for a few minutes, and then the door opened slowly. Mrs. Bunker was holding a small child, rubbing his back. "Did you come to arrest me?" She asked calmly.

"No, ma'am, but my partner and I need to come in. Who else is in the house with you?"

"Just the children," she said, opening the door wider. She glanced past Amethyst. "You certainly brought a lot of people with you."

"It's for your safety."

Amethyst and Talia went inside, closing the door. Everyone outside stayed in place.

~Claudia~

Daniel was particularly fussy all afternoon. He wanted his father, and she could do nothing to soothe him. When the knock at the door came, she was rocking him gently, trying to get him to sleep.

When the woman on the other side of the door spoke to her, Claudia realized she would have no choice but to let Kyle go. Her heart felt as if someone was choking the life out of it. She let them in, still holding Daniel.

One of the women who came in moved around the house, checking the rooms while the other kept an eye on her.

"How did you find me?"

"We triangulated your last call to your husband. He has no idea that we're here. I meant what I said. I'm not here to arrest you. Our priority is to get you and the children to safety. You may be in danger. Once we return to Dallas, Kyle will be removed from your care. We need to compare his DNA to the woman we believe is his mother. If the tests are conclusive, Kyle will be placed with her."

"And if he doesn't match her, what happens?"

The woman looked away from her before answering. "He'll be assigned a court advocate and placed in foster care until we can locate his biological mother."

"Why can't he stay with me?"

The woman sighed. "Because of what you did when you took off. Taking him and disappearing is something a judge would be afraid you'd do again. I'm sorry."

Claudia felt stupid, but there was nothing she could do to change her actions, and she wasn't sure she would change it if she could. "Fine, but you'll make sure that he's taken care of?"

"Of course I will. Now, we need to gather your things and get going. Talia and I will drive you back to Dallas. Half of our party will accompany us to provide protection in case we need it."

Claudia hadn't brought much into the house. She was ready to leave in less than thirty minutes. She got in the back seat of her car with the boys while the agents spoke with the rest of their team before joining her in the car. A very small part of her was relieved, but more than anything, she was sad, thinking of how her family would have to adjust to this change.

~Sameera~

When Sameera got back to Kenny's house, it was after nine. She hoped that Kenny was still awake. She missed him, and now that they had been intimate, she couldn't imagine sleeping upstairs with her sister. She wanted to sleep snuggled close to him.

She stepped into the house, hearing Haimari shouting, "Take that!"

Kenny grumbled, "I should've never taught you how to play this game."

Sameera moved past the entry to peek into the living room where their voices came from. There were bowls of chips and dip on the coffee table and a few plates.

"Have you guys been playing video games since I left?"

They both turned to her, grinning. Her sister turned back to the game, but Kenny stared at her, smiling. He mouthed, "I missed you."

Sameera crossed the space between them, leaning over the couch to kiss him. Then she told him, "I missed you too."

He turned his attention back to the game. "To answer your question, we have been playing since you left."

"Yeah," Haimari added. "He thought that he would beat me because I had never played, but I'm a natural at this."

Hippo glanced at Sameera, grinning. "She's only winning because I have to play one-handed. When I'm all better, we'll see who beats who. How did everything go?" He asked when Haimari fired the shot that killed his character.

Sameera moved around the sofa and perched herself on the arm beside Kenny. "It went great. We found Mrs. Bunker and the children in an old ranch house still in her father's name. I feel sorry for her. She loves those kids with everything in her. I can't imagine being in her shoes. Mike and Cougar are driving back with her in her car. They kept some of The Beasts with them, but a few of us returned on the plane Gopher arranged. Did you know that he's a pilot?"

Kenny shook his head. "Whenever we used a plane to get somewhere, he always rode in the cockpit, but there was usually another pilot there, so no, I didn't know."

"Well, this was one of those small planes, and he flew us there and back without assistance."

Haimari got up, picking up the dishes and trash on the coffee table. "Thanks for the game, Kenny. Maybe we can play tomorrow. I'm going to clean this up and let you do whatever," she said, taking what she had in her hands to the kitchen.

"I was hoping you would sleep in my room now, but if you want to stay with Haimari, I understand."

"I want to snuggle with you," Sameera said as she slid off the arm of the sofa. "But first, I want to change out of my clothes."

"Okay, I'll meet you in the bedroom," he told her, grabbing her hand and pulling her close for another kiss.

After he let her go, she went into the kitchen. Haimari was at the sink. "I already know. I get the bed to myself from now on."

Sameera grinned. "Yeah, you do." She moved around the counter, kissing her sister on the cheek before going upstairs.

Chapter Forty-Three

~Hippo~

The next few days felt like a dream to Hippo. He and Sameera were having difficulty keeping their hands off each other when she wasn't training or working with Haimari on the idea of a public outreach program. Haimari wanted to have the details nailed down before she spoke to the club about sponsoring and supporting her vision.

His collarbone was feeling better, and he had a follow-up with the doctor to see if he could stop wearing the sling. That would make his life so much easier. He still had three weeks to go in the cast, but he was barely taking the pain pills he had.

He spoke to his mother on Friday when she called to remind them about the celebration at the church. She also wanted him to make sure that his club brothers, who gave their time and energy to fix the leak, would be there too. Hippo wasn't surprised when they all responded that they would be there after they got the text invite that he shot off to them a few days before the party.

Saturday was a beautiful day. The sun was shining, and it was already beginning to warm up, though. In Texas, it could be seventy-five degrees one day and freezing the next. It didn't matter. The party was being held inside.

When they arrived, he realized his mother had invited some neighboring businesses and homeowners. Mr. Moon and the woman who owned the hair salon across the street from his shop were there.

After greeting his mother, Hippo spoke with the Pastor, who wanted to thank him for facilitating the repairs. Haimari was talking to Panther on the other side of the room, and Sameera was talking to Mr. Moon,

Carl and Eden arrived, and he introduced them to his mother and the Pastor. His mother fell instantly in love with their daughter, Destiny, practically kidnapping her from Eden. Sameera came back to him, holding his hand.

"I was beginning to think that you were going to dump me for Mr. Moon," he told her, squeezing her hand.

"Not a chance," she replied. "He was telling me he wished your stepfather Darren could be here. Mr. Moon told me the whole community admired him for raising you as if you were his own kid."

"What are you talking about?" Hippo asked, confusion clearly displayed on his face. "He wasn't my stepfather."

"Maybe I misunderstood him," Sameera said, mirroring his expression.

Hippo looked away from her to Mr. Moon, who was chatting with Haimari and Panther. The barber wasn't senile or anything. If he said that, then he must have a reason. "Excuse me," he told her as he let her hand go. "I want to clear this up."

~Sameera~

She wasn't sure if she should follow Kenny. Sameera had apparently opened a can of worms. She

261

watched from across the room as Hippo extracted the older man and moved to a quiet corner. The two men exchanged words calmly, but the look on Hippo's face told her enough. He didn't know that Darren wasn't his biological father. She began looking for Dottie in the room. She was still holding Destiny as she spoke to a small group of people, including Carl and Eden. When she turned her eyes back to where Hippo and Mr. Moon were, Kenny was coming towards her.

"What did he say?" She asked when the wheelchair stopped in front of her.

"He apologized; he thought I knew by now. Other than that, all he would say was that I needed to talk to my mother about it. Which I plan to right now."

Oh, no! Sameera turned, following Kenny as he headed for his mother.

"Excuse me," he said, interrupting her conversation. "Momma, can I speak to you alone?"

"Sure, baby," Dottie said, handing Destiny back to Eden.

Sameera wasn't sure if Kenny meant that he wanted to talk to his mother alone or if he wanted her there for support. "Kenny?"

"I'll be back in a minute, baby," he said without looking at her. Sameera turned to Carla and Eden with an awkward smile as Kenny and Dottie moved away from everyone. He led her to the Pastor's office and closed the door once they were inside.

~Hippo~

The minute the door was closed, Hippo asked, "Who is my biological father?"

His mother's response told him that Mr. Moon was telling the truth. His mother's shoulders sagged, and she let out a breath as if she were relieved. "We don't have to do this right now. Let's talk about it after the celebration."

Hippo shook his head. "No. We need to do this right now. It was you who lectured me about keeping secrets just a week ago. Let's get this out in the open. According to Mr. Moon, the community admired your husband for raising your kids as his own. Tell me the truth, Momma."

His mother turned, moving one of the chairs to a position so she would face him eye to eye. She sat down, taking his hand. "Kenneth, I wasn't always a good woman. I went through a phase where I rebelled against my mother and father. I was fifteen when I met your real father. He was exciting and different. We got involved, and I got pregnant with you. My mother and father put me out of the house, and I went to him. He got me an apartment and paid for everything I needed, but it wasn't how I thought it would be. He had several girlfriends, and I was just one of many, but by the time I figured that out, I was pregnant with your sister. As soon as the doctor confirmed it, I got this vision of what my life would be like if I continued being involved with him. I would end up on welfare or working myself to death with a house full of kids that didn't mean much to him. Don't get me wrong, he loved you and your sister, but he wasn't the one-woman kind of man. I realized that I needed and deserved more. I met

Darren while trying to figure out what to do. I asked him for advice, and he admitted that he cared for me and offered to give me a home and help me raise my children. His only requirement was that we raised you both as his. That meant your real father would have to step back and give up any connection with you. I didn't think that he would do it, but Juan conceded and did just that, but before he did, he told me that he would do it because whether I believed it or not, he loved us. He just didn't want to give up his life for ours. He knew he couldn't be the man he was, a hustler, drug dealer, a lady's man."

"Juan, who?" Hippo asked. It couldn't be the man he was thinking of. There were a lot of Hispanic people with that name.

"Juan Garza," his mother said.

Hippo let her hand go and sat back in the chair. "My biological father is the biggest dealer in South Dallas? The same guy who sent his people to stop me from selling pot in the area when I was a teenager?"

"Yes, and he did that because I asked him to. I've been trying to keep you from becoming just like him."

"Why didn't you tell me any of this before now?"

"I was trying to keep my promise to a good man who loved you with every fiber of his being. You may not share DNA with him, but Darren was your daddy. When I told him that I didn't want any more children. He accepted it and poured all his love into making sure that you never felt like you weren't good enough. In his mind and mine, he was your father. Please forgive me for lying. We just got over my prejudices where your club friends are concerned. I don't want to lose you again."

Hippo was hurt by the length of time he was lied to, but he tried to put himself in the same situation. If he met Sammi and she had children already, he would be willing to do the same thing for them because he loved her that much. "I forgive you, but I want to meet Juan face to face. I think you both owe me that much."

His mother nodded. "I'll arrange it."

"Today. I want to meet him today."

"Alright, I'll call him right now," she said, getting up and grabbing the phone's handset from the desk.

"I'll be out there. I'm sure Sameera is worried about what's happening in here," Hippo said, moving to the door.

~Sameera~

While Kenny and his mother were in the office, Sameera tried not to stare at the door. She talked with Carl and Eden. Then she cruised the buffet before sitting in one of the chairs lining the wall by the entrance to the sanctuary.

The door opened, and she practically exploded off the chair, moving towards Kenny as he came out. "Is everything okay?"

The smile he gave her didn't reach his eyes. "It will be. Turns out that my real father is the area's biggest drug dealer. It's a long story that I'll tell you later."

"Where's your mother? Are you two going to be okay after this?"

"I told her I wanted to meet him, so she's calling now. We're going to be fine. I understand why she never told me, but I want to talk to him myself."

"I'll be with you when you meet him if you want me to."

"I'd like that very much," he said, grabbing her hand. "I love you."

Sameera smiled before kissing him. "I love you too."

Coming in the next edition of the Road Beasts Saga:

Panther begins falling in love with Haimari while becoming friends with Michelle, who is struggling as a parent when she gets her son back.

Hippo meets his father and learns that he has other siblings.

Cassidy tries to dig deeper into who the Beasts are and finds herself becoming more attracted to Goose.

Raja spies on the Bhatt sisters but learns the hard way not to mess with them.

And more.

All of my titles that aren't in KU are available in ePub version directly from my website for less than you will pay on Amazon. Check it out for yourself.

Ways to keep in touch with me,
and follow-on social media

About The Author

Kimberly Smith was born in Aurora, Colorado, and raised in Dallas, Texas. Nothing about her life has ever been simple or easy. She was raised by a single parent who was visually impaired. Kimberly always had an active imagination. This creative imagination led her to a life of crime. Eventually, she was caught and served time in federal prison for a white-collar offense. During that time, she regained her love of reading and writing.

Kimberly's experiences have shaped who she is throughout her life, and she is grateful for her "federal vacation." Without it, she would not have known of her illnesses and would not be alive today. She has survived cancer. She thanks God for giving her a second chance to dig deep and understand what life is about.

Kimberly enjoys watching The Walking Dead Franchise of shows and snacking on gummy bears and flaming hot Cheeto's while letting her imagination run wild. Most of her stories have been in the interracial romance genre. With a love of unbelievable fiction, she is expanding into mysteries, science fiction, and paranormal writing.

Keep up to date on what she is working on at https://www.creativeKRS.com

Made in the USA
Middletown, DE
30 April 2023

29749398R00156